DRIFTWOOD

Aled Lewis Evans

*Drif*twood

Short Stories and Monologues

Aled Lewis Evans

bwthyn
GWASG Y BWTHYN

ISBN: 978-1-907424-04-5

This book is published with the financial support of the
Welsh Books Council

Published and Printed in Wales by
Gwasg y Bwthyn, St. David's Road, Caernarfon, Gwynedd LL55 1ER

CONTENTS

INTRODUCTION

Many thanks to Martin Davis of Afiaith for working on adaptations to English of the original Welsh language stories. This is with the exception of Highlights and The Café monologues, adapted by myself. The Café was first performed in the Wrexham Arts Festival of 2006.

I hope this selection of my work will be of interest to new readers, and will also serve as a bridge to my other published works in Welsh over the years.

Many thanks to Gwasg y Bwthyn for publishing this collection, and to Geraint Lloyd Owen for all his assistance.

Aled Lewis Evans.

Highlights

Regulars at the café had sensed that something was going on. A few had noticed that there was a little more sparkle in Sue's eyes when she saw Garry. A mother's life could be exceptionally busy with four children and an unemployed husband with the blues at home. Sue worked in the afternoons, and certain evenings at the café – cooking, clearing, and washing dishes – an extension of what she did at home, without the children and her husband's long face.

She should have had fewer children. She made sure that her younger sister got to know about the Op that the men could have to make certain of that. She didn't want Claire to be in the same rut.

Garry was like a warm ray of sunshine shining into the middle of the bleak monotony of the afternoons, He'd come to ask her how she was. Nobody had asked her how she was for years.

Garry was in his forties, single now, and used to years of looking after himself following the divorce. He was the resident Casanova at the Llay British Legion Club – a bit like Tom Jones with a Sex Bomb in his eyes, but without any of the knicker-throwing.

Whenever he entered the café you almost expected a spotlight to come on accompanied by the music of "It's Not Unusual", and for middle aged women to start showering him with their undergarments. However he was a gentle, quiet and cultured man, who had missed his chance in life really. Life had just slipped through the cracks. He'd had far more people taking advantage of him, than the other way round, despite his 'Oldest swinger in town' image.

He was a runner, although the good old days at the Queensway Running Club had come to an end. The memory and inspiration of succeeding as a member of a club had meant a lot to him inwardly, and glimpses of this could still be sensed in the corner of his eyes when he was not consumed by the glare of his own ego. The good old days of running the London marathon; and before that climbing the Welsh peaks, each one in turn – Aran, Arenig, Cader Idris, Tryfan, Y Grib Goch, and Snowdon. His physique remained fit and agile; he was a 'young dresser', and his attitude to life seemed far younger than that of a guy in his late forties.

The whole thing was considered a bit of a joke in the beginning, when Sue would bring over more pudding for Garry, or let him order without queuing at the till. That gave her the excuse to go over to him, to make sure that he kept her a seat during her break. He was faithful, and came to the café every day, and was becoming a constant and necessary part of her life. To make light of the whole thing, Garry would threaten to move his patronage to the Little Chef or Sainsbury's if he didn't get his scone at a cheaper rate.

Garry became a daily customer at the café, where at one time he had only been an occasional visitor, and Sue would often work evenings, as the Arts Centre café never closed before nine. Garry brought the frivolity of a schoolboy back into her life, and she almost believed she herself was back in the Groves High School.

Choosing a cake from a tin Garry would say

"While you've got it out, I'll have one as well, as the actress said to the Bishop."

Cups of tea, cigarettes, and life experiences were

shared round the table, and the usual gang still came and went, shadowing and greeting them, and yet knowing full well that there was more than an attraction here.

Sue started looking better – she no longer carried the worries of the world on her shoulders, the pressures of the café were easier to manage, and she coloured her hair with golden streaks, blonde highlights, as a celebration. This gave her an unusual radiance and lift in her work behind the counter, and many remarked how well she was looking. Often the gang would go home leaving Garry there waiting – perhaps to take her home in his brand new white XR3 outside.

Three months later, with her four children gathered round her, clutching at the buggy like the instruments of a One Man Band, Sue had been doing a bit of the morning's shopping from Iceland. Despite their being in the midst of the bustling crowds under the Arch by the Horse and Jockey, people couldn't help but notice Sue. Her smile seemed more certain and natural, despite all the demands being made on her by the children.

"I haven't seen you in the Cafe for ages, Sue. Where have you been?"

"I'm not there now am I? Don't you remember that I got the job in the garage in Rhos-ddu? Three pounds an hour for less work than the café, and I'm sitting down! It's like going for a rest after being home with the little ones. I've got to release the petrol pumps for each customer, and look after the money. But that's not a problem, because I used to do the till every night in the café. It's a busy place – but the time goes quickly – and we rent out films and DVDs, and it's a bit of a shop as well. It's a different kind of rush compared to the mountain of washing and drying clothes, and preparing meals at the café. It's a bit of an eye opener for me as well, as I've had to learn how to use the computer."

11

"You look well. It's funny without you in the Arts Centre."

"How's the old gang?" She paused a few seconds to prepare her eyes.

"How's Garry keeping? Remember me to him when you see him. He was a kind man."

The conversation was punctuated with the echo of shoppers' footsteps on the pedestrianised zone, and then by the voice of the eldest girl.

"Come on Mam, let's go and get it!" she said emphatically.

"She's going to the Big School next week; aren't you?"

Sue straightened herself.

"We'd better go and get Melanie's brand new school uniform then hadn't we children?" she said lightly turning to go. "I'll see you. Look after yourself. Remember me to the gang."

Her last sentence was meaningful but incomplete. Remember me to Garry was what she really meant.

As she went to turn the corner her old customer at the café noticed that the light blonde highlights which had adorned her hair weeks earlier, had nearly faded, and grown out. Only the slightest traces remaining on the fringes of her experience.

Framing the Shot

The usual bundle of early morning mail thudded onto the floor in the hallway of the Shelter for the Homeless. Harry was there waiting. He searched through the post for what was his before anyone else was up and about to filch them. It was the time of the month when all the photographic periodicals would arrive. It was a highpoint for Harry. Back in his cramped little room, he would finger the vibrant pages assessing the latest range of cameras on the market.

Photography was Harry's life. A total passion and obsession. He would bend the ear of unsuspecting victims in public places, to expand in great detail on how much he liked that particular camera or this particular lens, and how cheap film didn't really pay off in the end, especially if you had to use lighting. One of the walls of his room at the hostel was full of magazines all parcelled up and stacked like wallpaper.

After a good breakfast, inspired by the magazines, Harry fetched his own camera, checked it over, snapped it shut, and then headed out for another day of viewing the world through his lens.

Harry had been unlucky. Someone had ransacked his flat in the Spring Lodge area, stolen most of his property and set the flat on fire, destroying his entire past which was recorded in newspaper cuttings and photos. Luckily he stored most of the area's local history in files in his memory.

He had to be out of the hostel every morning before nine. One of the rules for staying there long-term. That's why his day would begin so early. Usually, the shelter only accepted short-term clients until the Council could find them somewhere, but the Council were dragging their feet with Harry. Everyone dragged their feet with Harry – but there was a place for him in the Shelter for the Homeless. He came there after a few evenings of sleeping rough in the shadow of the smart-looking chapel nearby.

One more picture and then it would be time for coffee. It was never too early for coffee for Harry. Tall, thick-lipped with his camera slung over his shoulder and a cumbersome plastic bag in his hand Harry struggled along towards one of his favourite haunts. He walked with an ungainly authority in front of the Racecourse football ground with the early morning traffic spraying him as it hissed past. Suddenly, a man came out of the ticket office and before he was able to go any further, there was a sudden inexplicable flash in front of him. It was one of the club officials and he was not in the mood in these unhappy times for the club, to be the subject of an intrusive lens.

"Listen, pal, what do you think you're doing taking pictures of me?"

Harry hesitated, dumbfounded by the idea that someone might not want their picture taken by him.

"It's just for myself."

"Take any more an' I'll deck ya."

Instead of answering, the photographer merely raised the camera to the man's departing back and took another shot. Seconds later the official's car screeched past at a reckless speed, while the photographer seemed to be pondering whether he had managed to get a good shot or not. There would be plenty of other opportunities during the day. He replaced the lens cover.

His mother's death had been a dreadful blow to Harry. He had lived then with his academic brother until he too had died. But there was very little communication between them in the narrow confines of their terraced cottage. Then a friend came on the scene, and this friend succeeded in channelling all Harry's money to his own ends, leaving Harry a destitute shell of what he had once been. The friend invested the money he purloined wisely. He then built a beautiful mansion for himself in Penymynydd leaving Harry to wander with his camera and his dreams through the shabby deprivation of the big town.

Harry would spend his days reading the newspapers in the warmth of the library and taking a few pictures while his friend would occasionally entertain him in his palatial residence – a rare chance for Harry to get away from the monotonous regime at the Shelter.

A good half-hour after the incident outside the Racecourse, Harry walked into the coffee shop at the Library for his ten o' clock coffee. This was a popular venue which Harry particularly enjoyed because photographic work by his internationally acclaimed contemporaries would be on display on the walls of the art gallery. He threw himself into one of the wobbly plastic seats, immediately disrupting two ladies from Marford indulging in the sanctity of their daily coffee and gossip ritual. One of them pointedly rubbed her nose. Their morning session of putting their little cream-cake-world in its place had been rudely interrupted. They turned up their noses as they left at speed and Harry in turn took their picture.

One of the waitresses came up to him.

"How are you this morning?"

"Grand. It's alright in between, isn't it?"

"Yes. You're busy with your wotsit, are you?"

"Quite busy," he replied, not wishing to divulge too much.

"You'll want the usual to keep you going?"

"Yes please, and a slice of coffee cake like the ladies. No cream."

He reached for his camera and aimed it at the food counter.

"You're not going to take me again. Your house will be full of photos of me."

She went on to ask him whether he had enjoyed the lecture the previous evening – she was well used to dealing with him. Yes, he had enjoyed it but the lecturer had gone on a bit. A woman in the café had told her that Harry had been yawning in a loud and anti-social manner in the middle of the lecture and that some people had actually started to laugh. The young lecturer had heard the sound at the back of the room and although it didn't seem to impinge on his performance, he had noted this breach of common courtesy and when Harry came up to him to take his picture at the end, his response was angry.

"Who are you? What do you want?" No reply, just a flash. "Who are you taking these pictures for?"

"Only myself, like. I like to take snaps of celebrities when they come to town even if the are a bit boring."

By the end of the morning Harry had found his way to Yale Hall – the local mansion opened to the public to show life both below and above stairs in past times. He had never managed to get a crowning shot for this location.

He had known the old squire years ago. He remembered walking over fields to see him, and finding sheep in the back garden. It was hardly the same now, under the aegis of the Trust.

One of the Guides nudged her co-worker.

"He's back again."

Their whispers fell silent under the photographer's impassive gaze. Despite his having been there several times before taking photographs, he went through the usual formalities.

"Am I allowed to take a photograph?"

"Yes indeed. Flash is also permitted here," came the well-rehearsed response.

His second question would be sure to unnerve the most experienced guide.

"Is it alright to use flash?"

The other guide nodded, and the first smiled nervously.

Harry dropped his Asda plastic bag with a resounding thud on one of the oak chairs, the din distracting the two rather posh ladies from Marford who had been in the café earlier, and who by now were admiring a piece of china in the corner of one of the restored rooms.

After a short while the guide who was busy discussing the piece of china with the ladies of Marford felt a light touch on her shoulder. She thought that it was perhaps her colleague wanting to add something to her spiel as she was relatively new to the job. However she turned mid-sentence to see the photographer and his camera framing a shot of her. Her relaxed manner turned to apprehension, as her face was suddenly illuminated by a flash.

"Lovely" said the photographer to the now silent trio.

Presently came another question.

"Can I see the tapestry rooms?"

"I regret to inform you that the Tapestry Rooms are closed to the public this morning due to repair work," replied the older of the two guides, who had now returned to the scene after dealing with an alarm in one of the bedrooms. One of a party of rowdy local schoolchildren had gone under one of the ropes, and she'd given them a piece of her mind.

"Well what a pity." He made a face like a sad clown. "No tapestry today?"

The nervous smile of the guide suddenly gave way to a display of temper, despite her years of experience. She had reached the end of her tether.

"Tell me once and for all – what are you doing here?"

"Pardon?"

"Well you roam round here all hours of the day. What do you want from me?"

"I want to get the picture right."

"What picture?" she asked, snatching his camera from under his nose. "What do you want here?"

She opened the case.

"Look it's an old thing to start with. How do you expect to take a decent photo with this? There's even a crack here."

The photographer didn't move an inch, he merely contemplated the scene in detached amazement, pursing his lips, as if he were about to kiss the irate guide. She opened the back of the camera exposing the contents.

"And everyone everywhere knows that you haven't even got a film in the camera." She held it out for him to see for himself.

Silence.

Harry gazed at the empty apparatus. Gingerly he took it from her, fingering its cold mechanical fragility. His pursed lips started to tremble, and tears came to cloud the focus.

The Call

It had been a very strange Christmas Day. Gareth had been sent by the local radio station where he worked to the hospital to talk to the patients and nursing staff about their 'White Christmas' and their remarkable enthusiasm away from home on this festive morning. However, despite the tinsel and carols there were also tears. On the wards Gareth came across Welsh-speakers isolated in an alien environment, decorations in their hair, yearning to go home. In one corner, a woman asked him to write a note to her bank manager in the village. Her daughter had not shown up to see her.

'I'm tired and I want to get home to sleep in my own bed.'

'Oh look, she's crying,' observed a cruel voice in English from the other side of the ward where two women were busy opening their Christmas presents.

'Still, Our Saviour's with us, and I'll keep praying. But I *am* tired...'

Her words stayed with the radio presenter as he hurried back to the studio.

It was six o' clock on Christmas Day evening when Gareth finally ventured on air at the end of what had been a quiet day, complete with microwaved Christmas dinner in the studio. There was hardly anyone around. Only himself and his edit tape and another presenter in the main studio. The news team had departed in a flurry of farewells around two in the afternoon.

Who was going to turn the radio on at this time with everyone busy drowsing off the effects of the seasonal blow-out? Would there be anyone out there, ensconced in their bastions of plenty, who would welcome the Christmas message? He wondered whether the carols and other talk items would touch the hearts of anyone in the catchment area today. To Gareth in the seclusion of the studio, it was difficult to believe that anyone was actually listening.

As he played the first record of his programme, Gareth was reminded of that lonely presenter who had sobbed on air simply because he would be continually giving out without receiving anything in return. Christmas evening was such a time for a lonesome broadcaster and Gareth could easily empathise with the unhappy presenter in question.

Is there anyone out there listening – anyone at all? Do you like me? If I were to knock at your door tonight, would I get a welcome? Would you take me into your embrace at this joyous time? If I asked you to phone me during the programme, would you respond?

For weeks the station's staff had been promulgating the jamboree that is Christmas to their local audience with talk of fine seasonal foods and wines on air. Santa chatting with the little ones, and Boney M moidering on about the Baby Jesus with as much conviction as a deflating balloon. By now, the creators of this Christmas carnival had retreated into their private lives in search of some sense of the true festive spirit, leaving Gareth broadcasting alone ...

Was there anyone listening?

As the tape played on in the studio, Gareth went to check if there was anyone around. Not a soul. Only his voice spewing out of the speaker rattling on about Christmas and the Faithful in these adverse times.

A silent blanket of snow, which had appeared

stealthily while he was busy preparing out the back, now lay over the panoramic view from the studio window. It would be tricky getting home tonight. The snow was something of a surprise. The road had been clear that morning and none of the forecasts had predicted it would be like this. There were no technicians around on Christmas Day and Gareth knew it would be better to go back to the studio. Silence on the airwaves would be an embarrassment requiring a credible explanation to the station director after the holidays.

He opened the heavy studio door. Limp strands of tinsel hung from the sound boxes along the wall as if it had long since grown tired of its rather pathetic function. Another record on the turntable. A cuppa – the ultimate panacea. He rushed out to the little kitchen, but the kettle was stone cold and the remains of the midday microwave banquet lay submerged in the treacly waters of the sink. A swig of the insipid dregs of lunchtime wine seemed hardly worth the trouble. His only link with the outside world since that morning, had been Ray, the landlord of the local pub, bringing him his Christmas dinner to heat up – stuffing and all the trimmings, it being Christmas.

It was time for the final record – a ballad about a telephone operator trying to get Jesus on the hotline to heaven. As he listened, Gareth stared at the row of lifeless phone lights linked to the studio.

'Well, this song longing for Jesus to be at the other end of the line brings our programme to a close this evening. It's just been me here for most of the day, but on behalf of the company may I wish you all a very good night and a very Happy Christmas.'

Following the final chime of the station's Christmas jingle, he set about putting the studio to bed, turning off the required switches. Gareth then started off the pre-recorded tape which would run leisurely through the

21

night and set about clearing away the records and tapes from the studio. He was worried about starting the car in the snow. The song *Jesus on the Line* stuck leechlike in his mind, and he found himself whistling the melody as he was leaving the studio.

In his haste, he failed to notice that one of the numerous phone lights was winking away, obscured from the door by the tinsel. It was the emergency line to the studio flashing wildly – someone wanted to make direct contact.

May I Have a Little Bit of Blue Sky Today?

The radio studio was a hive of activity. Everyone rushing to and fro looking for an empty studio to record some item or other, or to grab a spare moment somewhere else in order to finish off work on some tape or other. A non-stop rush and bustle.

Ruth had been a great help to Alun on his Welsh language programmes being the only Welsh speaker in the building apart from himself. More or less since joining the station she had been doing an item on the nightly Welsh language slot, talking about any events taking place in the area. They'd have a lot of fun recording these and tapes containing all the bloopers and gaffs were carefully preserved for some suitable occasion – material for a special Christmas tape perhaps!

But Ruth hadn't been recording the Events item for several weeks now, and somehow she'd become more difficult to pin down to get her into the studio. There was less incoming mail to be answered too. It was a combination of circumstances which had meant that things weren't quite as usual, without anyone having intended it.

At last they managed to get Ruth to the studio, despite her muttering something under her breath that there wasn't anybody to answer the phone and that she'd left someone totally inexperienced – one of the Job Creation girls – in charge in reception.

"We'll get it done in a jiffy," said Alun, as he set the tape running.

Stop

'Did you realise you said *Edyrnion* instead of *Edeyrnion*. It's *Côr Merched Edeyrnion.*'

"I can't do them like this. I haven't had a break. My throat's parched. I just can't do everything, you know.'

'Would you like *me* to do the Events? asked Alun innocuously.

'So you don't want me to do them then!'

'You know I want you to do them, but I don't want to have to go on my knees every time to see whether you're prepared to do them or not.

Ruth went ballistic.

'Right, that's it. I've had enough. I'm going to speak to the boss about this. I've had it up to here,' she yelled, hurling the Events' schedule towards Alun. She had expected him to follow her as she stormed out – but, to her great disappointment, he didn't.

Ruth was just about hitting middle age. She would get her hair done in Chester almost every week and wore loads of make-up. Sometimes she could look old, as if her youthful bloom had faded once and for all; at other times she would seem to be eternally young with her features and skin looking as fresh as a woman many years her junior, and her eyes sparkling behind her glasses.

After the incident in the studio she headed straight back to her own territory in reception, without so much as a glance towards her colleagues behind their desks in the open-plan office. She clawed for her coat, bag and umbrella.

'Ruth are you all right?' enquired one of the girls in the sales department realising that something was wrong.

'I'm going! I've had a enough! That's it! I'm off and I'm not coming back.' She pushed her out of the way.

'No … I'm going.'

Ruth strode home, crossing the busy main road to the estate where she lived. Her history was too long and complicated to bear – she just had to get out of there and get home. Home was her ultimate refuge, and as she got into her nightie and lay in a stupor on her bed with the sheets pulled up over her head, the big bad world no longer existed. That was the philosophy which governed her life with regard to both the past and the more recent breakdown of her marriage.

'I won't think about the past and then it'll be like it's never happened.'

Under the sheets, the only hope she held out for the big bad world was that she would hear a knock at the door. That would be the signal that she had won and that the rest of them had had to come to her. She remembered when she was little – the eldest among her siblings. She'd often had to look after them and take them to the beach, as if she were their mother. More often than not her own parents would be quarrelling. She remembered how one day she was by herself on the dunes at the edge of the salt marsh. Her brothers and sisters were playing on the beach in front of her. She was looking up into the sky. The sun and clouds were casting an ever-shifting pattern the length of the beach. She could almost discern faint echoes of her parents' quarrelling being carried on the wind. She remembered thinking at the time as she stared up at the sky that the little pocket of clear blue – such a beautiful blue – was slowly but surely being strangled by the clouds. She remembered longing for more blue, for more of the pleasure it brought and willing the clouds to go away. 'May I have a bigger piece of blue sky today?

And that was how her life had been ever since; whenever there was the slightest sign that the skies were going to cloud over and hide a bit of the sun, Ruth would come along and sweep them away whenever the blue sky was under threat using any number of different strategies. Soon, she knew there would be a knock at her door to show that she had won and that the sun and the blue sky were back in their rightful place.'

There was a time when Ruth had been overwhelmed by the clouds and she had had to resort to being in the care of medical professionals at the mental hospital. The clouds of her childhood had returned with a vengeance when her marriage broke down. For a while she actually regressed to being a mute infant, clinging on to her dolly as she scanned the skies for a patch of sunlight and a spot of blue.

The blue came back, but since that time she would chase away the black clouds with a renewed vigour. The mere hint of a cloud would trigger off a robust self-defence mechanism. She would take to her bed, seeking its neutrality or await an intervention from the phone or the front door bell. In her home she created a fortress of cloudless blue, and it was within the confines of this fortress that Ruth sought refuge after the incident at the radio station. And that's where she was, curled up with the cat – who never answered back, when the front doorbell rang.

In the meantime, Kathy the Sales girl who Ruth had barged past on her way home, came to talk to Alun.

'I know it's nothing to do with me, but have you just had words with Ruth?'

The outcome of this conversation was the deputation now ringing Ruth's front doorbell.

Upstairs the urgent note of the bell brought the outside world back to life in Ruth's ears with crystal clarity. She got up, put on her dressing gown and descended the stairs to where the blurred outlines of her visitors were visible through the rippled glass of the door. Kathy too could discern Ruth's shape through the distortions of the thick pane as she came downstairs.

'It's Kathy, Ruth.'

Ruth scrabbled for the key.

'Come in, Kathy.'

Then she saw that Alun was there too and she glared at him. But despite this charade she knew she had won. Although he had given way to her, she'd have to keep up the act in order to milk every drop of sympathy she could.

'You know how much I love doing the Events? I'm willing to do them for free. I don't get a single penny for them anyway. Don't you see how important this was for my self-confidence – after everything I've been through.'

Although the clouds had been sent packing and the sun was out again, Alun was not allowed to enjoy the sunshine today. He would be punished for allowing the clouds to threaten her horizon in the first place.

"Obviously not.'

'Well, you don't know anything about me then.'

Despite everything, she invited Kathy and Alun into the house for a cup of tea and it became apparent that the Events issue was merely the tip of a large iceberg of problems which had been building up and distracting her, like little bundles of unpaid exigencies on her desk in reception.

"I've had a row with the boss too, and now he's sulking in his office. He said that I'd hurt his feelings. But all I did was tell the truth and the truth always hurts.' She had swept her clouds towards him.

Quarter of an hour later, everybody was back at the office. Alun was flabbergasted by Ruth's behaviour, and she was conscientiously trying to placate everyone whilst chewing away on a *cornetto*. She was now staring at the pattern of clouds and blue sky outside as she tried to get her day back on track, even though she'd been so upset and was unlikely to do much work for the rest of the afternoon. The boss would be OK if she just kept on smiling and making cups of tea for him in his metal mug without any grumbling.

As Ruth knocked on the boss' door to start her afternoon with a cup of tea, she was called in.

'Sit down for a moment, Mrs Roberts.'

Ruth didn't notice the black cloud which had darkened the sky outside the office window. It hung in the air above the building, devoid of even the tiniest speck of light.

The Inscription

This was a rather different sort of Friday evening. Marged switched off the TV and relished the sudden peace which reigned in the living room. A Friday evening with her husband off down the Club for a pint with the lads and her under age son out down the pub for the first time, promising to be back home by ten; the girls, in the middle of their exams, were already in their beds. Marged enjoyed the occasional Friday night like this, usually in front of the box or doing a few household chores, or occasionally even having a friend over for a chat, Friday night was generally a quiet sort of affair.

She relaxed in the easy chair in front of the fire, motionless apart from the flickering flow of her memory. Her recollections would mostly range back along the highways of her life, but tonight, despite herself, she felt her mind turning down one of the back roads of her past. Normally this particular *cul de sac* was ignored in the general hubbub of life, but, nevertheless, it was a place which contained such vivid and painful memories, a place she occasionally had to revisit ...

She knew tonight that things would go further than the simple recall and non-recall of individuals. Tonight something was drawing her attention to the cupboard full of books in the far corner of the room, but it wasn't a reading book she was after this evening. There was something else in that cupboard, drawing her like a magnet, compelled her to shake off her sloth and get up out of her chair.

29

Marged wasn't a great reader, but throughout the twists and turns of her life she had received books as gifts and had even purchased the occasional title herself. In the cupboard there was a set of three handsome volumes containing the complete works of Somerset Maugham. She took out the second of these, fingering it reverently. The cover was thick with dust which she hastily blew off, as if trying to get rid of some trespasser who was threatening to violate some part of her – something deep down inside. We're all basically dust so they say. Marged didn't believe in dust.

She shut the cupboard door as if she were closing the door on someone's past. And yet part of that past was now gleaming in her hand. What secret did the book contain? Marged knew very well. She opened the cover and there it was. The words written there were more important than any of those in Mr Maugham's stories.

"To Dear Marged on her success in passing her nursing exams and at the beginning of her professional career. With all my love, Rick."

Rick was the book's secret. Rick who was so different, so sweet, so devout. Rick was the key to her success back then. He had spent hours revising with her, fixing the facts in her head to ensure her success in the gruelling exams ahead. And that success had indeed been spectacular.

She remembered Rick revising with her until three o' clock in the morning in his flat, and how the other girls in the nurses' home had joked about her, expressing strong doubts concerning the nature of this 'revision'. But Marged knew that Rick had never laid so much as a finger on her, and had he done so the respect and love she had for him would have disappeared overnight. Rick had love and patience and ability, and a black skin – a fact which had caused such shockwaves when she and Rick had gone home one weekend. Her mother had cried openly on seeing this giant of a black man coming into the house. Her mam wasn't so much opposed to the colour of his skin, just unable to comprehend, unable to cope with the situation having had no experience of it in rural Wales. It wasn't prejudice so much as ignorance which blinded her. However, eventually a mother's love prevailed and Rick was accepted if not with open arms.

Marged stared at the inscription in Rick's immaculate copper plate hand, recalling the occasion on which it had been written, something she rarely did these days.

Of course, after she married, she had to burn the photos, the letters, everything for the sake of her husband, but she kept the books. Her husband would never dream of reading Somerset Maugham. It allowed her to hold on to the past securely and without fear of discovery! This was not some foolish yearning for what was long past, but simply the preservation of a part of the life she had lived, to bring a certain thrill to those moments when she thought of Rick. She loved her husband to bits, but this was one place to which he was denied access.

Marged knew the whole sad tale. A letter had arrived at her home many years later to say that Rick had married happily and now had a family back in Zambia and a good job in the country's health service. The letter asked for information of her whereabouts. Her mother held on to it for months before admitting to its existence. Marged would have answered it but her mother refused to co-operate. What if her husband got to know about it? The letter remained unanswered, the communication remained one-way and the picture stayed incomplete.

Marged knew that Rick and his family had been killed by terrorists in their own country, and that they had been brutally tortured before being drowned in their own swimming pool, along with other dignitaries. She remembered her mother's words: "You see, love, what would have happened if you'd gone over there."

Rick and his family and the circumstances of their death were not overly mourned, despite being the subject of banner headlines in the newspapers, expressing horror at their slaughter.

Marged knew the strength of Rick's faith. His was the greatest spiritual and non-physical love she had ever encountered in her life. She had not found anything like it in her marriage, but she had found other things and had a fantastic family, and had come to accept that we cannot have everything we want in this life.

But she did have the book and nobody else in her family knew about it. It was a sweet secret, a memorial to a durable love, a love which would not grow old.

It was almost ten o' clock and before long her son would be back from his first experience in a pub in town, and a bit later on her husband would be home. Marged stood up and returned the treasure to the book cupboard to remain hidden for some time yet.

As she closed the cupboard, the front door bell rang. It was ten on the dot. Her son had respected her wishes to the letter. She ran to open the door.

Exile

Toronto,
May 1st 1980

Dear Alun,

I'm really sorry for being so tardy in replying to your letter – the contents of which I thoroughly enjoyed. I'd been thinking of answering with a long scholarly epistle similar to your own, but I messed it up and I ended up depositing it in the wastepaper bin. So here I am giving it another go.

I'm settling down OK on my own now, although the cost of living is going up far too quickly for my liking and I won't be getting any increment to my pension for another three years. It was doing Edna and me very well back in '77, but this runaway inflation has left me way behind. I've been asking around with regard to some light work in a postal distribution depot but they said I'd have to take my place at the end of the queue because I wasn't born here. Which basically means that some high school yobbo could get a slice of the cake before me!

I hope your parents are over their illnesses and are now looking forward to many years of good health and good spirits. Is your Dad still working? Tell him not to work too hard or the strain is sure to take its toll. That's what happened to me. Working non-stop with more work than I could handle properly within the deadlines.

Congratulations on getting your degree in French –

good for you! I'm very proud of you! It was worth giving it another go after all, wasn't it? Gwilym still keeps going, he wants to change his course and so on and is a bit peeved. He's gone off for a break somewhere.

I put flowers on Edna's grave yesterday.

Well, I'd better call it a day.

Wil J.

Long Beach
California,
April 15th, 1980

Hiya Al,

How are you, muthead? I've escaped to the West Coast with Dolly. Talk about high life. It's great, man! We're living together in a shack right by the ocean. Gorgeous place. Swimming every morning. We're in the middle of a heat wave here. Life is just one long joy-ride.

Cheers,

Gwil.

Toronto
Sept. 3rd

Dear Alun,

Just a brief note to thank you for your phone call a couple of weeks back when I was out with the dogs. What a shame I missed you.

I'm much better now, the treatment on my neck has killed off the melanoma and almost all the other has been removed. I'm taking loads of Vitamin C at the moment in an attempt to get rid of anything that might be left. It all happened so suddenly, didn't it? The X-ray isn't too clear.

The weather's been really lovely here, just like summer although the States have had a really bad time of it. At last I've got round to ordering a piece of sculpture for Edna's grave and I want to tidy up the plot a bit. Haven't heard a word from Gwilym; they say he's run off with Dolly – nothing but trouble there. I wonder where they've disappeared to for such a long time?

I was very pleased to get the book you sent me on the strict metre poetry. I'm starting to build up quite a little Welsh library here. I never saw such a thing in my life as that magazine you sent me from home, *Tua'r Ffin*. I've sent the cash but haven't had anything back yet. And they're asking for contributions too! A strange way to run a newspaper. I can't see what the problem is about sending a paper through the post. Someone needs a good kick up the arse, and if I was at home that's what they'd get.

I've heard that Vitamin C is really good against cancer – ten grams a day, if you can. I'm taking three grams a day now. I enclose a really useful article about it. You can never tell when you might need to know about this sort of thing.

Remember there's plenty of room for you to stay here

any time you want – as long as you help with the washing up.

All the best,

Wil J.

P.S. I enclose something towards the phone bill.

Long Beach,
California.
Sept. 15th, 1980.

Hi there, Al, me old mate,

I've just brought my dream car. Fantastic! It goes like the wind from one end of the beach to the other. Still based in California. It's been a fabulous summer. Not particularly keen to see the old man. I'm sure he's grinding on as ever. I'd better not.

Hey! Hey! Hey! Dolly is some gal. She's expecting a baby. Just think, I'm going to be the father of her child. Whoopee! This is just a really rushed note because I'm writing it half-stoned – it's Dolly's birthday, don't ya know! My head's stuck in some huge cloud at the moment – bit of a knee's up all round. I'm sweating like a pig 'cos it's like the middle of summer here.

So long,

Gwil.

Dear Alun,

It's like the grave here. There's nothing to do but look at the Christmas lights through the window. Nobody calls. Only the woman in the next flat to do a bit of shopping for me. I'm not sure whether she's moving out. She was talking about it. I can't really be bothered to make myself anything to eat. The throat's giving me hell – I can't swallow or eat anyway.

I'm sure I caught sight of Edna walking along the street. I waved to her but she shot off into the subway. You won't believe it! Mam and Dad came to see me yesterday; honest to God, I didn't think they knew where I was. I was always a bad lad. Mam made me a nice poached egg on toast with brown bread with a lovely lake of melted butter on it. And Dad sat in the corner with his pipe muttering away. You can still smell the smoke. They sent their regards. They were asking about Gwilym but I didn't want to show my ignorance. Perhaps he still lives in the old country but I can't for the life of me remember him.

Yours sincerely,
William John Jones

P.S. My citizenship came through at long last. I can hold my head up now.

Toronto
Friday morning, December 13th

Dear Alun,

It's real brass monkey weather here. Everywhere whiter than white and freezing hard. I'm almost frozen through myself. My throat feels as though it's on fire. There are huge floods on the roads and I'm stuck here. The electricity's down throughout most of the county. I'm having great difficulty talking these days – I can't get the words out properly. All I can manage is writing the odd note to yourself.

Tell me, is that old paper still going in Tre-ffin? What a rag it was too. I did have a bit of an urge to contribute something, but I'll leave it for now, wait until spring is in the air again.

I'd like to get home for a while. Just for a break, to see the woods at the Plas coming into leaf. I remember it all today. Every little detail. Gwilym'll be home from school in a bit, bless him. I'm continuing to get better.

W.J.

Toronto Police Department

December 14th 1980

URGENT TELEGRAM DELIVERY
To   Mr Alun Evans
      Fridducha
      Llanelidan
      Wales England

WILLIAM JOHN JONES DIED LAST NIGHT STOP NO KNOWN CONTACTS HERE STOP INTERMENT 16TH DECEMBER STOP YOUR LETTERS IN HIS WALLET STOP

Head of Police Department

Long Beach,
California.
Friday afternoon, December 13th

Hiya Al,

The baby's arrived. Terrific! Gwilym Davy Jnr. My God, how's the old man going to take the news?

Gwilym.

A Heart or Two

'Ten pence a go, on the best turntable in town – some old, some borrowed and one or two to make you blue', boasts the inscription on the front of the jukebox.

Certainly, every song has its history, each one meaning something to the regulars here. It can all be very revealing. Listen to their stories now as the needle drops into the groove... or whatever it is these days!

'TOO MANY BROKEN HEARTS IN THE WORLD'
JASON DONOVAN. (PLAYING)

I'm Kirsty. Jason Donovan. Glenn looked just like him with his beautiful fair hair. But then *she* came along, didn't she? And stole him. I really really hate her. I'll never talk to her again.

I thought she was someone from one of Glenn's bus trips, or from when he was a bouncer at the disco club, but she lives just a few doors away. I never dreamt... and she used to come over to ours and I'd be making her a cup of tea 'n everything. She used to cut the kid's hair, for God's sake!! Kelvyn and Kylie. She used to cut Glenn's hair too, and I didn't... she can cut it every day now if she wants to.

He asked me for a divorce, and I just cried for days. Mam came round and gave him a piece of her mind. What are you doing? You've got two wonderful little children? But I don't understand. She lured him away somehow. She wears nice clothes and so on, and she's got a good figure, but she's not what you'd call pretty. She's only twenty three and Glenn's thirty, you see. I've no idea what attracts them to each other. I'd like to know. You see, I haven't done anything wrong, and it's me who had to go to court and everything. It was terrible. I had to wait four hours before I went in. There's a hell of a lot of divorce around these days... and much worse than that too.

I don't know if I want him back – maybe he'd do the same thing again, if he did. It's always in the back of my mind. He's coming here now as if nothing had ever happened, and at least we're friends. To tell the truth, we're better friends now than we were before.

Kelvyn's not too bothered about his dad now and they're going to Spain on their holidays. Her uncle's got an apartment there. So it'll be cheap for Glenn, and they won't get any holidays from me. You know, I don't blame Glenn at all. To my mind, it's all her fault. I know I'll have to face her one day – at a family party, and it's going to be difficult. I thought I was going to see them together at my cousin's 21st. And I was ready to see them together, but they didn't come. Glenn was working nights and couldn't get anyone to do a swop.

My sister's husband's brother, Conrad, is hellish good to me, and Kelvyn likes him more than he does his dad to be honest. He's asked me out, but I don't want anything like that. I don't want any commitment. I want time to myself.

I've only signed from myself and the kids on the Christmas cards this year. I've been brave enough to do that.

'YOU WERE ALWAYS ON MY MIND' ELVIS. (PLAYING)

Hello there! How are you today? I'm Gwyn Owen and this is my corner of the Red Cow. This old number by

41

Elvis has me transfixed in my seat. I've been here a bit longer than usual tonight – people watching. A real patchwork quilt of characters. but whatever else about them, they've all been fine with me. And Margaret too, if it comes to that. I've got to know a lot of them from helping out in the greengrocers at the top of the street when the owners went off on their holidays.

This old bar stool is a very pleasant perch 'cos I can get to talk to some of the Welsh-speakers when they come to the bar – it's good to have a chat in the old language. And, fair play, nobody's against Welsh here. Hopefully, in my own small way, I can have a bit of influence on the English.

I'm not a great drinker, just so many halves, but tonight I'm staying here a bit longer than usual trying to talk to as many people as I can. You see, Margaret loved Elvis. Wasn't it strange thing, my losing her on that last Saturday before Mr and Mrs Karussis came back to the shop? I was totally stunned 'cos it had happened so suddenly, but everyone's been great here. I don't sleep so well on my own now. I'm all right until about four in the morning, but I can't get back to sleep after that

I won't be buying the *Gazette* again either; I'll tell them where to stick their so-called newspaper. I sent in an obituary notice three weeks back. They've got a column, haven't they? And I can't understand why, but it's only today it appeared, after waiting for the *Gazette* every Friday morning. But there were some who jumped the queue, didn't they? And some people who'd died after Margaret did appeared in it at the proper time. But not Margaret, bless her. I was on the phone with them a week ago, and I got an apology and a word with the Editor. But the following week, there was nothing in the paper again. There were only three death notices that time, and right above them a huge advertisement for four car auctions in the New Year. I got on the phone the day before yesterday and put that Editor in his place. "You should worry more about those who've left us, but all you care about is money. I don't know what the world's coming to. If we're OK and still buying your paper, everything's fine, apparently. Well, I'm not going to be buying your rag any more...

'I WANT IT ALL' QUEEN. (PLAYING)

Hiya, I'm Ali. Why me? Why not anyone else in this pub? I'm the one who always gets it. Why can't I choose someone sensible, someone just for me? It must be that I just choose the wrong type of man. No one else wants anything to do with me.

This is where I come to every Saturday night, making excuses to everyone. You'll have to excuse me but I've had a bit too much today. I always have a bit too much. I'll be in chapel tomorrow, mind, and everyone'll think I'm very different, but come Saturday night and I'm with the crowd down the pub, bumbling around the glasses, the fag ends and the men's eyes – and landing up in yet another human tragedy.

I've got no one else to blame but myself. Everyone says how I can't see any further than my nose, but I know what I'm doing. I should have more control but I can't stop myself. Most people have a soft spot but why do I try to reach out to people like this? But men are bastards. Why else do they leave my place at half past four. Men and their lies! Absolute bastards...

I'm always the last to find out the truth. Take Meurig for instance. How was I to know that he's fathered kids the length and breadth of Wales with different women? I'm not a bloody mind-reader, am I? He seemed a nice guy to me, who happened to come into the pub and I didn't know anything about his background. But a friend of one of the regulars knew about him and his history, his kids and his various wives. I gave him what for. I didn't spend any more time with him until half past four in the morning I'm telling you. He buggered off on his lorry on a long journey somewhere to make use of some other poor cow.

'OH YES, I'M THE GREAT PRETENDER'. (PLAYING)

Oh, yes, I like this one. 'Oh yes, I'm the Great Pretender...' We're all the same when it comes to love, aren't we? Blind panic if we don't find it, like moths round a flame. Doesn't time fly when you start thinking about where the last years have gone? I'll look at myself in the mirror sometimes and think. "Ali, what are you really like?' Who are you really? Can you look yourself right in the eye in a mirror? Does what you see honestly tell you everything about yourself? What's tomorrow got in store for this face? Will it find something good or yet more failure?' I hope I don't lose control. I couldn't face that. And all these lines of experience all over my face – it's not easy taking a good look at them and trying to feel content.

I'm still in the same hole. Take this specimen beside me here, on his way to drunken oblivion. Take away his tattoo, his earring and his hair style and what have you got left? Another sack load of lies. Another bastard. But he makes me feel warm for a couple of hours. He's got his past too – at least he's told me about that. A hell of a history too. Kids and wives all over the place, and he never goes to see them, selfish little devil. But there's something sweet about him deep down under it all, and yours truly is the only one stupid enough to believe that and to get myself hurt again.

But for a few minutes anyway, my life's not in bits all around me. As for the future well, we'll see. The next decade? Who knows? But for tonight I'm going to choose *Happy Christmas. War is Over* on the juke box. John Lennon and Yoko Ono. And if I look deep enough into his eyes hopefully he'll be mine again tonight. Half past four – or we might even get a lie-in!

Oh, the little prat, he's started taking off his trousers in front of everyone, making a proper show of himself. Why does he always have to do this when he's had a drink? The song's gone sour even before it's started.

'LOVE IS LIKE A BUTTERFLY' DOLLY PARTON. (PLAYING)

I'm Jeff, Jeff Jones from Ponciau and it's strange hearing Dolly Parton of all people. Quite amusing really. Malcolm, the guy I used to live with in Bournemouth, was a Dolly Parton fan. So I remember all her songs. He had all her LPs. It's strange how I still remember. They say that time heals, but I'm not so sure. Perhaps I'll forget one day.

Five years. It's a long time to have a relationship with somebody. After I'd found out he'd been unfaithful, no way could I stay there. It would have meant going past his workplace on my way to and from mine and we had the same friends. I just had to go. You don't realise just how great the loss is until they're not around. I couldn't engage with anyone, mentally or physically, as I had with Malcolm.

But two years have gone past and there are signs that things are getting better and that there's different criteria in place and we're friends again. Strange, how we used to take the dog for a walk on Christmas Day. I left everything – the video, the records and everything and cleared out and we'd worked hard on our home. We'd stripped all the paint back to the woodwork throughout. Time heals, but not completely. Never completely. But I couldn't stay. I had to leave my work as a window-dresser, leave everything. The job lot – and start all over again.

I'll go back one day when I'm strong enough, back to the waves and the beach and the cliff path. Back to face

Malcolm as a friend – him and his Dolly Parton records. Believe it or not, but this song's quite right – love is like a fluttering butterfly – uncertain and fragile, searching for an anchor or harbour before nightfall.

'ENDLESS LOVE' DIANA ROSS AND LIONEL RICHIE (PLAYING)

Hiya! I'm Deborah. I work in the clothes shop down the road during the holidays. You know the *His 'n Hers* one. I come to this pub almost every lunch hour, 'cos I'm at the Art College. I'm not sure whether I fit in there either what with everyone so busy trying to make an impression.

Hey! This song does something to me. There's much more feeling in the way black people sing, don't you think? It brings back memories to lighten the disillusion of a twenty one year old. You know there was a time when I felt as light as one of them birds which used to hop from clothes line to clothes line at the back of our houses. Then along came Chris. *'You never know when I'll pop up'*, is what he'd say, and now he's as far away from my heart as Timbuktu. And yet he's not so bad. Frightened to face himself and his feelings, that's poor old Chris' problem. He acts out life like all macho men do. You know the type, all brawn and no brain. If he could just let go of the mask and get to know himself, to like himself, he'd be OK. *He'd be good for God*, as Abigail, my friend from Bristol, would say.

He works at the pool in the Plas Madoc Leisure Centre. He gets plenty of attention there. He always wanted attention, never gave it. At the beginning I thought he was fantastic, like someone who come down from the planet Sbot scattering cosmic dust into my ordinary little life. I thought somehow that he saw deeper than the other – that he saw the 'me' inside of me as it were. There's a real Chris in there somewhere too. I got a glimpse of him before he disappeared and shot off back to Planet Sbot. I remember being able to talk to him openly, while I'm usually shy with other people. But it all gets hidden under this image which rears its head time and time again.

Money, money and more money! That was his thing, to keep that chunk of metal he swanks around in on the road. My heart still misses a beat when I see a similar car. Just in case. I thought he saw into me, right to the essence of my being, past all the superficial crap. Everyone else just responds to that. Chris was the only image that I've ever believed in.

Are you like me? There are people in our world we're glad to see that they're still around, still living from day to day, and yet, somehow, we're frightened of going back to their world, in case there isn't the same welcome in their eyes. You'll never know what sort of look Chris is going to give you – a distant look that's pleased to see you or else a look as if you didn't actually exist any more.

After I finished with him, it wasn't easy, but the pieces of the disillusionment jig-saw fell into place. It was strange the transformation from being a very special person in someone's mind to being just like anyone else. When you see someone after a long gap and you realise that the old magic has gone. Just a few words and then: "*Well, I'd better shoot off,*" – shoot off being the operative word in his case, to keep his image and his car intact. All he said was "*See you're driving a new car.*" I saw him a few days ago. "I'm sorry for not sending a Christmas card." Liar! Liar! I went out for a walk under the stars to clear my head of the lie. These image conscious types are always so lazy, however attractive they might be on the surface. There are no lies in the stars or the moon and the river, and it's to them I turned. My dreams were shattered like a glasshouse with hardly a single shattered shard of hope left.

I know I don't mean anything to him, I don't even come between him and his ego, and yet I'm prepared to listen quite coolly to his pitiful excuses. And he's got a cheek – asking me to call into Plas Madoc if I wanted a bit more of a chat. Ha! That would be a laugh with his lordship ignoring me in the middle of all his busy-ness. I heard from Trish that he's *playing the field again* – his own description. If only his natural side could flourish and if he could just let the image drop. But no, he's a coward. Him and his bloody cars! He thinks more about his cars than he does of people, working every hour to keep his beloved car going, but doing nothing to work on a relationship. I don't understand him. I'd like to go over to his place with a stone and scratch all the paint off that car, just to make him realise that there is so much more to life and that a car can't feel. I don't mean he has to take me back, I'm not the answer to his dreams, but he definitely only sees half the show, like Cliff Richard sings in that song *Time*. And talking of Cliff, it's him on the jukebox now...

A LITTLE IN LOVE, CLIFF RICHARD (PLAYING)

Oh my God, look whose come in. I didn't expect to see him in here tonight. Here's me having taken weeks to calm down and get me head sorted and then he waltzes in, all smiles and excuses. Chris. And the juke-box has gone quiet...

Happy New Decade everyone. Twelve o' clock chimes out and everyone joins hands in time-honoured fashion for *Auld Lang Syne*, out on the street, everybody hand in hand. The dance of the nineties shaking Kirsty, Gwyn, Ali, Jeff, Deborah and Chris into facing the future.

The Border

Just think what could have happened! The tyres screeched their protest against the curb and the whole vehicle lurched alarmingly. Osian had closed his eyes for just a split second – but it was enough. It was high time for him to get some sleep.

Surely he must be nearly home by now. He slowed down and tried to get his bearings. He couldn't work out exactly where he was. He glanced at the petrol gauge. The needle was well into the red. Damn and blast! He was almost out of petrol – yet again! He was in his usual pickle on his journey back to north Wales.

He saw a light on the left hand side of the road. A powerful light at that. He slowed down and came to a halt. Hopefully, there would be someone there who could let him have a drop of petrol, and give him some change for the ten pound note in his pocket. He wasn't so far from home, but it was pitch black and he didn't fancy being stranded on such a cold and dark night and having to walk along the verge to a garage.

As he got out of the car, Osian felt the icy grip of the night air. The chill was particularly noticeable to him as he had only just returned that morning from the summery warmth of Israel where he had been recording a radio programme, straight into to the depths of winter on the Welsh Marches. He had been up since six and the stresses and strains of his recent expedition were starting to kick in.

He approached the house where the light blazed from a downstairs window. He rang the doorbell and knocked several times, but all to no avail.

Unsure of what to do next he caught sight of a glimmer through the hedgerow a bit further along the road. He returned to the car and drove slowly along the verge until he came to farmyard entrance.

The light he had seen was above the front door and it was easier for him to head towards it than to try making his way round the back of the house which seemed to be in complete darkness. He went through a gate and across a small patch of lawn and garden towards the old front door. The door was rather unusual. It looked quite ancient and forgotten and seemed to be in a rather fragile state-of-repair, as if it were more for decorative purposes than anything else. He knocked tentatively.

Through the thick glass he saw a shadow and heard someone approaching.

"There's someone at the front door. Nobody ever comes to the front door." said an elderly man's voice in Welsh.

Thank goodness, thought Osian. They're Welsh. The shadow withdrew either in fear or to open the back door. Osian knocked on the glass again.

"Yoo-hoo!"

A voice came from the depths of the house.

"Hello?"

"Oh, hello. I'm sorry to disturb you but I'm almost out of petrol."

Suddenly the door flew open.

"You speak Welsh! In this part of the world? And you've run out of petrol? Come in, lad."

The elderly farmer led Osian into the cosy depths of the house. There was an air of antiquity about the place – with its grandfather clock, its dark woodwork and low ceilings. He followed the old man into the kitchen where the woman of the house was sitting by the fire. Against one wall a dresser was jam-packed with crockery, photos of grandchildren, and, judging from their attire, pictures of two sons outside the farm on the day of their graduation from college.

The old man explained to his wife what had happened.

"You'll have a cup of tea, won't you?" she said, delighted at the opportunity to make a fuss of a visitor who spoke her language. "It's so unusual to find Welsh speakers in this part of the world these days."

As she made the tea, the old lady chatted to Osian while her husband went to sort out the petrol for the car.

"We're the only Welsh speakers between here and town. The only ones. You wouldn't believe it, would you? In front of us there's mile upon mile of marcher woodland. They're like soldiers caught between two worlds, I always think... We get Welsh on the wireless, but we don't get it on the telly – we have to put up with bloomin' *Channel Four UK*, if you please. Do you see the photos on the dresser?"

"I'd been looking at them," answered Osian.

"My sons were in prison, you know? And Glyn and me were right behind them every step of the way. We agreed one hundred per cent with their stand. They climbed up one of the masts and refused to come down. Just imagine it... I didn't like thinking about my boys locked up in prison. We had to go to the court in Liverpool and all we were asking for was justice..."

She passed Osian a framed photograph from the dresser.

"These are my sons. It's strange to think that they're all living in England now! By choice! And the grandchildren don't get a fair crack of the whip with their Welsh. Here's a picture of them in their graduation clothes by the old front door. The one you knocked on tonight."

She turned to face Osian and paused in the middle of

cutting and spreading a thick layer of butter on beautiful homemade *bara brith*.

"There's no need for that front door really. We're the only Welsh speakers on the border, and that door faces straight towards England. When I'm in the house and Glyn's out in the fields, I get to feeling that I'm the only Welshwoman left on the planet. Glyn's here with me, but, you see, this house faces east and the enemy's all around us and closing in all the time. It's a chilling old border. We go westwards to the chapel every Sunday, and get right away from having to listen to her old whispering.

"Who's that now?" asked Osian.

"The old border. But I won't give in to the old witch. I can hear her breathing at the bottom of the garden. Sometimes, I think she's disappeared and we've got the better of her and we can relax. We can pretend she's not there. That she's never existed. Sometimes on a fine day I'll go out to sunbathe in the garden and listen to *Radio Cymru* as loud as I want. We haven't got any neighbours here. Just her. But on days like that she disappears. But when evening comes, she'll be back, laughing away, and there's me thinking I'd managed to get rid of her. But we refuse to give up. Glyn and me. We refuse to give up."

By now Osian had pitched into the refreshments which had appeared like manna from heaven on the kitchen table, helping to revive his flagging spirits. The old lady continued with her story.

"You know, sometimes I feel the border is scratching away at that old front door, outside ready to suck us away. She's so full of mischief and charm, just like the devil himself. I sometimes hear her breathing hard as if she was beginning to lose her mind. But other times she'll be wandering away."

Because of his tiredness, by the time Glyn got back with the petrol, Osian decided it would be best for him to get straight back on the road.

"Thank you very much for your kindness. I'll get straight on my way again if you don't mind.'

Two days later after buying a suitable bunch of flowers as a token of his appreciation for the kindness shown by Glyn and his wife, Osian decided to nip over to the farm in a break between two sessions in the radio studio. But despite searching the length of the main road along the border, going from one farm gate to another he was unable to find the farmhouse with its mysterious front door – the last Welsh outpost on the border.

The Form

The chill December air and the seasonal warmth of the Post Office building clouded its big windows under a veil of condensation.

The focal point of the office was the clock, which beamed down constantly on the heads of the bustling businessmen in their lunch hours, and the frail pensioners dragging themselves to the counter under the glaring welcome of the strip lighting. The place was full of the usual cacophony of footsteps and voices – the hustle and bustle at the door, the sound of a pram being manhandled up the awkward steps, the usual murmur of complaints as the next queue along seemed to be getting better service ...

Behind the glass partition the staff, craned forward towards the narrow slits in the pane which allowed the customer's voice to filter in.

"Give us two First Class."

"Do I have to sign on the dotted line?"

Some of the staff would sit there like high court judges, staring snootily at the shameless shirkers signing for their dole. However, for most it was a case of constantly being on the go with the service in full flow – a continual flicking from page to page in the stamp book, and tearing the fragile perforations. Or else their heads would be down, their ears straining to catch the muffled requests and queries at the grill.

The staff was as hybrid a workforce as you would find anywhere. Old and young, men women, some of them very prim and proper; others somewhat more relaxed and informal... such as the young man serving at one of the windows who sported a large, piratical gold earring which came as quite a surprise to a few of the more elderly customers while they waited for their pensions to be counted out.

There was one other member of staff who was a bit different too: the Welsh speaker – Mati Hughes, who, at this particular moment, was watching the condensation dripping slowly down the huge windows in front of her. For a few brief seconds there had been a lull in the otherwise brisk trade at her booth. For a few precious moments, she managed to forget the damp well-fingered sponge, the carefully arranged pile of parcels and the never-ending pension and dole payments, and allow herself to drift back to last summer's Eisteddfod, back to the things which really interested her. At least in the *Gorsedd,* Welshness meant something, but here in an office full of mockers and scoffers, it could easily sink without trace in the tide of Anglicisation and ignorance.

Expressing her Welshness had often led to fierce spats with her colleagues, which they found very amusing but which upset her far more than she dared let on.

She turned away from the steamed up windows and contemplated her fellow worker sitting next to her at the counter. He was a Welshman – but one who spoke no Welsh and felt nothing for and knew nothing about the language.

However, despite all the provocations and her deep misgivings, Mati remained tolerant. She valued her fellow members of staff as human beings, and as part of life's rich tapestry. This was more important, she felt, than wrangling about the language. At times, however, she would still say some things – instinctively almost, the words forming unwittingly on her lips and tumbling out before she could stop them.

She looked forward to her conversations with the town's scattering of Welsh speakers when they arrived at the grill in the partition, and sometimes when she saw a Welsh name on a pension book or a form, she would be daring enough to ask the individual in question a little bit about themselves and how much Welsh they spoke.

"I would have liked to have learnt Welsh," was the response of most of the older generation, but the youngsters were more challenging and their shameless apathy would be like a physical blow to Mati Hughes' gentle features behind the glass, chilling her like the biting frost of this December morning.

"Don't insult me, for God's sake. Welsh? What use is to you, anyway?"

"You'd be surprised," she would reply quietly and return to the world of sticking the English monarch's head the right way up on the mail, without revealing the hurt caused: "I was just wondering, that's all."

Another cause of anguish in Mati Hughes' life was that her son was at present serving time at the pleasure of that same monarch – in prison – although not without his parent's support. The initial pain however had by now turned to joy and solidarity in her mind with the advent of the Welsh language television channel, Welsh on road signs, and even more particularly, Welsh forms in her workplace, confirmation that the heartache had led to brimming success. At least this would make the harsh reality of working in a very English establishment a bit easier to cope with and to accept.

Her reverie was interrupted with the arrival of a man at her window wanting to order a new driving licence, and his accent fitted the category Mati thought of as being unmistakably Welsh speaking ...

"*Prynhawn da*," she greeted him in Welsh. "You're after

a new driving licence then?" she continued in the same language.

'Oh, there's posh Welsh for you!" retorted the man scornfully in Welsh. "*Driving Licence* is what I say not that... whatever it was you called it. 'You're very posh with your Welsh, aren't you?"

"You have to fill in all of this side of the form," continued Mati, apparently unabashed.

'Don't think for a moment that I'm one of your Welsh Nationalists or in the Free Wales Army or anything like that. I'm going to fill in the English side."

"You don't want a Welsh form then?"

'No,' followed by a contemptuous laugh.

He pushed the money under the screen and Mati Hughes felt tears in her eyes. She certainly didn't want the man on the other side of the counter to notice and get the better of her.

"Well, remember this," she said as she passed him his change, "the next time someone asks you if you want a Welsh form, that some of our children have suffered in prison to get forms for people like you..."

The man looked totally bewildered and departed as meek as a lamb on receipt of his bilingual licence. Mati felt the tension releasing its grip on her body. She wasn't sure whether she wanted to laugh or cry now.

Suddenly there came a raucous voice from behind her.

"Get your skates on, Blodwen. Coffee time, or should I say '*coffi*'."

In the staff room as she sipped her *coffi* from her Red Dragon mug, Mati realised that she was having to spend her life making one futile stand after another. However, she couldn't help but chuckle to herself. She was glad that she had been able to find the words to speak her mind to the man with the licence. It would be easier next time. As the coffee warmed her, 'Blod' the old indomitable Blod, knew that justice and equality were on her side.

She laughed again before returning to the counter and taking down the "Closed/Ar Gau" sign to face the rest of the afternoon and the patchwork quilt of characters who made up the inhabitants of this border town.

Just a Few Seconds

Rhiannon's Confession

The memory'll prod at my conscience for just a few seconds, just enough to wake up the little skeleton somewhere in the dark cupboard of my subconscious. I'm able to control it now to just a few seconds – incredible actress that I am! It used to fill my thoughts for minutes at a time ... well, hours ... entire days actually – before the rift, that is. The rift with my youngest sister, Naomi. Before Naomi ceased to exist. But she can still call by on occasion, every day – just for a few seconds, mind.

Where is she these days, I wonder? What's she doing? She must still be living in the same place. Wrexham, that most English of Welsh towns which has so spoiled her. Naomi was always spoiled. And she's certainly always been odd – very odd. And now, whenever we get together as a family, we talk about Mam who's eighty six and as fit as a fiddle, and Beth, another of our sisters – divorced – a hell of a case though. But there's never a word about Naomi. She just doesn't exist, and we mustn't make her exist, even though she does – in Wrexham. And 'exist' is the operative word. She's broken off totally, hasn't been home for over four years, even refusing to speak to the next door neighbours in the council house, stubborn little so-and-so. Had some sort of an argument with them. But the whole family's stubborn isn't it? From Mam right down to my little sister.

'Don't play with those naughty children and then they'll go away. Just ignore them!' That's the advice I give to the kids every day. This is so true about life, isn't it? There's a Naomi in the class at school – there is, honest – like a constant reminder, and I do get to thinking about our Naomi every time I see that lovely name – N-A-O-M-I. And then there's this new teacher arrived from – guess where – Wrexham! Why couldn't he come from … Mostyn, for God's sake? It's hard since the rift. Very hard. We just have to try not to think about her. I can remember the names and faces of some of the very first kids I ever taught in Liverpool, remember them so clearly – it's just a pretence saying I can't remember Naomi. But the memory is blurred. Yet another excuse. I'm always going on about the release of atonement in chapel, but there's no atonement here, no release – only on a superficial level.

Naomi didn't even come to see her father when he was so very ill. And she was his favourite. She didn't come even when Mam wrote to her. Perhaps she moved out of reach, out of our reach. We're not all to blame, surely? We know where she is, but we're all scared. It was a really dirty trick, not coming to the funeral assuming she got the letter. Didn't want to face us. She was never like us lot, she used to say, but she was my little sister at one time. I remember when I was in college, doing a case study about her for teaching practice, and she was nine at the time and very bright. Naomi aged nine. I can face the past when she was a little girl and playing hospitals down by the river, or Cowboys and Indians. I was always the cowboy …

Her kids are grown up now, but we've never known them. Jamie – there's another name that goes right through me. That's her son's name. Perhaps I'll bump into him sometime. Although I avoid Wrexham. I avoid it just in case I might … have to face … just in case the seconds start turning into minutes, or hours, or days again. The fear after the rift. I must stop thinking about it.

Naomi *was* different. She married some guy for his money. English he was, and then got herself divorced. He was a nasty piece of work, apparently. We all have to put up with nastiness, don't we? Except Mam. She just couldn't bring herself down to that level – her daughter speaking English in Wrexham, turning her back on everything she'd been brought up with. I try to live a good life, know my place, in the chapel and the community, and at school, but there are moments – at the most unexpected of times – when I remember Naomi, when she comes to fill the emptiness she's left.

Perhaps after Mam dies it may be a bit easier. But will Mam die happy – completely happy, I mean? She won't admit her failure with Naomi. Threatening to cut her out of the will and everything, and she needs money more than we do. She's a bright girl, mind. A schism – that's what it is. An uncompressing rift – totally at odds will our beliefs, me and my husband – it's out of our hands. It's at times like this I start questioning what are we like; what act are we trying to keep up. As good an act as anyone else's, I suppose. When those moments take over then every sand castle comes tumbling down, until they're forced back up again by life as it is. I know she'd talk to me if I went to see her. Perhaps I'll give it a go in the summer, during the holidays … go with a note to the bookshop in Wrexham, asking for some obscure title, to see if she'd know me. Perhaps I'll go before that …

I wonder if anything or anyone will come along to repair the rift? Perhaps God'll come along to fill these seconds … minutes … seconds. He'll come if anyone does …

Naomi's Confession

What's come over me thinking about Welsh of all things? I'm not really its number one fan and that's for sure; I've got better things to do with my life than saving the language like my sisters and Mam do. Oh my God, I've admitted to myself that they exist. I've obliterated my memory of them, see, my background, my family, everything about them so that they don't exist for me. I haven't got a Mam or sisters. They're just so narrow-minded, so hellishly narrow. I didn't want to live like them. But I couldn't give two hoots, to tell the truth. They never came here when I needed them – them and their blinkin' religion. OK, so I married a stupid prat an' had a baby while I was still at college. I never got to be a goody-goody teacher like my sisters, although I pretended I had been … a teacher, that is.

Who the hell knows anything about my business in Wrexham anyway? After my marriage went down the pan, Mario comes on the scene, doesn't he? Jeez, he was a nasty customer – a real bastard and I divorced him too after I had his kids. They – the *Gestapo* back home – don't like the English names – Jamie and Wayne. Stubborn old Welsh goats that they are. It's not home to me anyway. Home wasn't the right word for it. It doesn't mean anything to me. Not a thing. I know its awful that I don't have anything to do with my family but I've got my reasons. There's no second chance there. Once you've blotted your copy book, they remember forever, out there in the Wild West.

And they couldn't stand *him*, could they? Number 3. Mr Dave Curtis, born 'n bred in Llan Fastening, if you please. That could have done the trick for them, but they refused to come to the wedding! Couldn't cope. They just couldn't get their heads round the fact that I was seriously looking for happiness. They just couldn't cope with someone in the family marrying for the third time. I can't stand north Wales. It's not like the south. People don't say what they think. Where I come from they just drop hints. Anyway, the buggers didn't come to my wedding, so I made sure that I wiped my memory of them, and they don't exist anymore. I can do without them, without their religion, without their language, without anything to do with my background. The little chapel girl – well, look at her now.

I still say I come from Criccieth, and I can still find my Welsh when its useful to do so, but I haven't taught it to the kids. I just don't want them to know.. I'm not so stupid that I don't know what I'm doing. Mabinogion an' all that. Blodeuwedd. Creating something with no roots, well, why not? I tell loads of lies to wind the buggers up – like saying I've started my own business – like hell, where would I get money like that? Talking all about my teaching experience – I've never taught in my life. I say I've got loads of friends in Wrexham – I can count my friends on the fingers of one hand. But I do have Dave. Nobody knows anything about me here, and anyway who's likely to know anything, I keep well away. I can get away with stuff here and then act just like my sisters when I want something or like remembering how to speak Welsh when I want to. This Christmas I've got a bit more cash than usual – running my own business in Bersham – and I'm goin' to get a video camera to film Jamie's little girl. I've told 'em they mustn't go to see Nain and the family, but after I told them all about them, they don't want to go anyway.

I was Dad's favourite and I didn't even go to his funeral – work that one out. No one's going to get to understand me.

Every time I hear the name Rhiannon, I never think of my sister, I just think of a friend of mine in London. She had a really nasty sister too and she would always be thinking about her friend instead of her sister. They didn't show any interest in my kids over the years. Only when I was dating that boy from Anglesey. He was Welsh, and they started to visit a bit then. But it's up to the kids now – not that they want to do anything about it – not now that I've spoken to them.

I was happy enough until I was about ten and then I began to feel that I wasn't like them, that I wasn't really their sister. I've got married to Dave now and I've changed a lot since I met him. I'd have preferred to have a family with a Nain and Taid they could see and aunties and uncles. But not that lot. Not after the split. I'd like to go home and have Mam welcome me with open arms. But she wouldn't anyway. They're totally unforgiving that family. But Rhiannon's the worst. She's worse than Mam! She's so scheming and hypocritical. It's alright for them to be Evangelicals and masons and whatever, but where was their Christianity when I needed them. For about five or six years now I've told 'em I don't want anything to do with them.

It's hellish ironic that I've got the bloomin' Gorsedd stones right by me, reminding me of Eisteddfods and Wales, every time I take Lisa Marie, that's my little grand-daughter for a walk in the Park. They just loved the bloody Eisteddfod, didn't they? Dave's a writer – I'm sure that would go down well too.

Nobody's going to find out the reasons for the rift. I don't want to waste another second of time talking to anyone. Every year, I promise myself I'm going to carry on just like this. Like some old witch. I don't need people like them in my life. I've got enough nice friends around, without them and their old Welsh stubbornness. Like me – although it's a bit different. I'm nice to people for different reasons to my family.

Christmas is the only time I start thinking. Mother's Day doesn't worry me at all. At Christmas I go all quiet, and have to retreat to some out-of-the-way café, as if I was ashamed about something. I usually go to the café near the church – the new one. Nobody knows me there. Everyone else is with their families and I'm there. But this Christmas I've got the video camera. But the rest of the time I don't give a toss about them.

The Gulf

She had a sudden yearning to go to the National
Eisteddfod, and to hear a children's choir sing *Unwaith
Eto yng Nghymru Annwyl*. Despite her present exile in
Wolverhampton and being married to Dave the gasman,
and despite having brought up her children speaking
English, the desire to be whole again was very strong.
The Eisteddfod was visiting her home territory – the
town of Mold – the town where she was born and
received her Welsh-medium education, the town where
she was given a start in life and the town she was obliged
to leave behind her.

It was not that she had been involved in all the
preparations; she knew nothing of the great surge of
activity and the years of hard work that culminated in
this one week of cultural overdrive, it was simply that a
relative had mentioned that the Eisteddfod was being
held at Mold and she suddenly felt the urge to be there
on the field, meeting up with old acquaintances. She had
been living beyond the pale for a long time and it had
been a good few years since she had seen many of her
friends.

Dave would come with her every year to stay in West
Kirby, and the children would be free to run around on
the beach and have gorgeous Park Gate ice cream and
take a day trip to Southport and make the inevitable
visit to see relatives.

There would be plenty for them to do while she went
off on a trip down memory lane.

It was an important day for her – although no one else knew about it, apart from Dave of course. A day of quiet recognition for herself. She caught the bus through Sealand and Queensferry, along the new road to Mold and from there to the Eisteddfod field. She recalled how some of her friends at school came from this close-knit industrial community, while others came from the rural areas to the west.

Her first port of call on the field was the *Siwgr a Sbeis* stall for an enjoyable snack to set her up for the rigours of a full day at the Eisteddfod.

So far she had seen hardly anyone she knew, just the occasional glimpse of some of her former teachers in the distance, usually wearing some official badge or other. She didn't like to impinge and anyway they might not remember her and everyone would feel very embarrassed. So she continued to observe and absorb....

By a strange co-incidence, two local actors were presenting a show that day in *Theatr y Maes* – an adaptation into Welsh of a piece by Alan Bennett concerning the boredom and loneliness experienced by two very different women in their contrasting environments – the wife of a minister of religion and a woman who wrote poison-pen letters. Melys felt she would like to see the show, particularly as one of the actors, Siriol, was an old friend going back many years.

The theatre filled up quietly as she waited for the one o' clock performance. She suddenly found that another of her old contemporaries had come in and taken up a seat right beside her. The newcomer however didn't seem to recognise her.

"Hello. It's Nia isn't it?" She felt a surge of nervous excitement as the words tripped out. "Do you remember me? I was in the same year as you at school. Melys Parry, from Lixwm.

67

"Oh yeah, kind of," came the response in a lazy English drawl and then "*Shwmai 'te?*"

"Still going."

There was an uncomfortable pause. Melys persevered.

"I've only come to the Eisteddfod for the day and I saw that Siriol was acting in this play, and I came to see what she was like – as an actor."

"We're on the caravan field, a couple of friends from the Beeb on either side."

Nia hated the ritual inquisition of the Eisteddfod field – questions like "Are you here for the week?" She preferred to get her retaliation in first.

"Siriol's a nice woman, isn't she?" continued Melys contemplatively. "She's done well for herself. I always remember her long hair."

There was no response from Nia.

"I haven't seen her since school…"

"I see her quite often in Llanishen," Nia cut across her.

"Is that in Cardiff?"

"That's where S4C is based. I work for S4C in Cardiff."

"What? The Welsh television channel? Television? Oh, that's why your Welsh is so good. A different story with me, I'm afraid. But you weren't from round here originally, were you? Somewhere in the South, wasn't it?

There was another uncomfortable pause.

"We can't get it where we are – S4C, that is. In Wolverhampton. Does Siriol do a lot of acting then?"

"She's done a couple of things for S4C. Minor characters in dramas, that sort of thing."

"Is she married?"

"That's her husband over there. He's an actor too. He's the one who's translated this play and he's helping with the props. Gethyn's a good sort. Always very willing to help out."

"What do you do, then – with … um… the Channel."

"I'm with the international programme commissioning

department. You can get S4C on S4C Digidol now – even in Wolverhampton!"

"Wow! It sounds like an important job. Are you like a sort of secretary?"

"There's a bit more to it than that."

"Are you married?"

"Yes. We've got two children – Osian and Lowri Mai."

"Wow! How do you find the time? Nice names, too. Pretty. Mine are Jamie and Toni. My husband said there wasn't any point in giving them Welsh names – they'd be difficult to say in Wolverhampton. They have enough trouble with Melys... and Dave's English anyway."

"My husband can't speak Welsh either, but the children are getting Welsh-medium education."

"You're tougher than I am then. What does your husband do?"

"He works for the Channel too."

"Oh, I thought you had to speak Welsh to work there."

"He's working in the graphics department. There's so much to do now with digital coming on line, and subtitling. He's learning Welsh anyway and promises total submersion at some point."

"Where better than the Eisteddfod?"

"He wasn't able to take his holidays at the same time as me this year."

"It's nice tho' – that you both work in the same place, isn't it?"

Yet another uncomfortable pause.

"My husband's a gasman. A very dangerous operator! He's staying with the kids in West Kirby today so that I can come here. He said he might go on the ferry from New Brighton to Liverpool and take them round the Albert Dock. There's a really good museum with the history of the ships and everything."

"Wouldn't it be better to bring them here to learn about their own history?"

"Well, he didn't know whether to come or not. It's an all Welsh festival, he says to me and turned up his nose at it. Perhaps I want him to turn his nose up. Keep today just for myself. He's so good with the children, but sometimes, I do regret that they haven't got any Welsh. If I lived in Wales it would be different."

Nia was just about to make some cutting remark. when one of their old teachers, who was now an HMI, began to welcome the audience to the feast of dramatic delights that was awaiting them that afternoon.

The performance lasted an hour. Melys thoroughly enjoyed it and was glad that she had seen her old school friend get an opportunity to act in such a wonderful role. Nia, however, did not feel that Siriol's performance warranted all the applause it received – particularly as she had snubbed her earlier when she had gone backstage to see Gethyn. She had to see him. She couldn't even go for a week without speaking. The stupid little bitch would have to watch her step. Did she have to spell things out to her again? Take the edge off her big performance? There were too many people always writing scripts with Siriol in mind as the main character. Nia had tried to stop some of them – but stupid bitch or whatever, she knew how to act.

Melys was brave enough to stay on at the end as everyone rushed out into the bright sunshine.

"Are you going to stay on to congratulate her?"

"No, I see enough of her down in Cardiff."

"Oh."

"*Hwyl,*" and Nia disappeared backstage to look for someone who was more worthy of her conversation; someone for her to suck up to with regard to future career prospects.

Melys held on limply to her coat and bulky Eisteddfod programme as the theatre emptied. She wanted some sort of positive connection with her past today, for the future – her future. Something in her had stirred after years of putting Wales to the back of her mind., almost denying it as part of her experience. It now seemed strange to have stored a language away in some secure recess of her memory without ever putting it into practice. The Eisteddfod field on her home patch was as good a place as any to establish this new link. She wanted to tell Siriol that she had been at school with her and had been part of that school family on the border, and that she could belong again. After a few minutes voices came from the wings and she rushed forward as Siriol emerged, her head bowed.

"Siriol! Do you remember me? Melys Parry from Lixwm. We were both at the Welsh school together. Oh... don't cry. Come here ... your performance was great."

The 'Oompah' Party

"Which is the guy who's just got married?"

"The one who looks like Groucho Marx."

The Crossville Club on a Saturday night on the fringes of the Maesgwyn side of town. Guests gathering for the evening party – an 'oompah' party, for the simple reason that the bride and groom insist on shouting 'oompah' before every photo in order to get everyone smiling.

"Hey, mate, is it you who's doin' the disco?"

Fire doors flung open everywhere, a sign of the heat generated by the wedding breakfast earlier in the afternoon. At the door, the bride, in her white wedding dress, accepts presents from young girls she doesn't even know with a grateful smile. In his element following a sweaty afternoon's carousing, the groom presses the flesh profusely, shaking hands with all and sundry, his arm resting on every available shoulder – things he would never dream of doing under normal circumstances. Basically he's a nice Anglesey lad...

"He's nothing like Groucho Marx."

Everyone moves on to find a seat and Hettie yells out from the corner.

"He doesn't remember us. Sailing past with his nose in the air. Chrissie's mam and dad."

"Who's Chrissie? Oh, Chrissie, she's so like you. This is Chrissie's brother, I take it?"

"No. This is Roger – you remember Roger, don't you?"

Chrissie's life story is then regurgitated to all those who care to listen and there's a garbled instruction to phone about eight on Sunday evening if you want to catch her in. Let's have a little 'oompah' before you go?" More photos and thank you's before retiring to the corner.

An argument breaks out – should the lights be kept on or turned off now the DJ's arrived. The disco comes to life with excerpts from new versions of the Twist and Simon Says. A taster. There's a bit of rather random dancing – it'll be better after the food. Where is the food?

"What are you drinking? Apple juice?"

"Yeah, I'm driving."

"Lazy git! You only live just round the corner."

The bride's uncle – the one nobody gets on with – smiling away as if butter wouldn't melt in his mouth and his wife with her orange juice at his side. The bride fights her way from table to table, taking the obligatory 'oompah' pictures, but really dying to take off her wedding dress and, in Mae West's inimitable words, 'slip into something more comfortable'.

The winner of the most Boring Man at the Party award is sitting with his head bowed, his wife trying to live his life for him, begging him to do the twist – "*And it goes like this.*" But there's no go in him. He turns his back on the whole childish charade of taking 'oompah' photographs – high time the bride grew up, he thinks. Their young cousin just can't stop dancing with the willowy and rather attractive June, who is bound for Australia tomorrow to start a new life.

Then there's a crowd of young lads who get quite a shock when who should walk in but 'Sir'. The youths suddenly become very restless with their pints. How does *he* know the bride?

The sweet little bridesmaid in her flowing dress is now rather tired and rushes to take refuge on her dad's knee

– namely The Most Boring Man at the Party who is himself almost asleep by now.

Poor old Uncle Bernard, the bridegroom's father's eldest brother, is wandering round with his video camera, shouting 'oompah' at everyone, lighting up some dark alcove or other and giving Auntie Hettie a bit of a shock!

'The old goat! He hasn't called to see her in years. He's calling by often enough with that gadget of his tonight tho'."

By now the wife of the Boring Man is trying to rock around the clock. The bride's sister is dancing frantically on her own on the dance floor and Auntie Hettie is enquiring anxiously whether she's all right. You've got to admit, it's difficult to tell whether she's a boy or a girl.

The little bridesmaid and her mam are now singing, and she's going to be on the video with dad sleeping soundly in the background.

The DJ, after a suitable 'oompah' greeting and having predicted that the "roof is going to be well and truly raised in Treffin tonight", announces that the food is ready. Everyone rushes to the buffet table to overfill their plates. Both bride and groom have to jump the queue in order to get food at their own party.

"Who said you could start?"

"Me," says the wife of the Longest Face in the world.

"Oh! Alright then."

While there is sufficient light for everyone to see their food, Uncle Norman from Rhosneigr fusses around taking photos.

"Don't worry if the pictures in the dark don't come out," the bride's sister consoles him. "You're OK. I've got a flash, see. Take one of me now, just in case. Oompah!!"

Everyone tucks in to the wonderful feast, and the bride's mother blushes at the torrent of praise from all sides. The pasties are really lovely – She made them all herself.

"Try one of the cones with real jam and cream. That would cost you 60p down in the café," urges the wife of the most boring man. The food rapidly disappears and the disco is back in action again, warming up like the gin flowing down Auntie Hettie's throat. The lights are turned off and the oompahs have fallen silent for the time being. The bridegroom is in his waistcoat and wearing his belt too tight showing off his belly, or concealing it, depending from which angle you happen to be looking. He's chatting with the woman whose nervous and yet happy to go to live with her sister in Adelaide tomorrow.

"I'm sure you'll like it. Down Under," he whispers, his hand wandering even before the ring is cold on his finger.

The poor wife of the most boring creature in the entire universe is still trying to persuade him to move his stumps towards the restricted dance floor.

"Do the locomotion… without me… I'm fed up of you," she snaps. "I'm going to the toilet to look for a bit of fun. On her way, she disturbs the bridegroom's youngest brother, Fireman Sam, snogging Ziggy in the tiny wet corridor outside the toilets. That's one fire that's not going to be put out tonight.

'Y *Viva Espania!* is the next song and the whole place comes alive. The fat niece who nobody really knows is reliving the hopeful discos of Benidorm and leaping madly around the tiny dance floor. The younger sisters are all laughing at the silly bitch. A chance for another 'oompah' picture are drowned out by the strains of the Conga. Auntie Edna, who never dances but who's glad she's come tonight, wraps herself around the bridegroom's midriff, surprised that he has so much to squeeze Down Under. If you can pinch more than an inch, has always been Edna's watchword…

The conga progresses both inside and outside the club, with the train of assorted relatives one-two-three kicking their way past a rather stunned Fireman Sam and Ziggy Stardust who are still snogging away in the manky passage by the bogs.

"Oompah!" cries Uncle Norman from Rhosneigr taking their picture leaning on the red fire-extinguisher.

'Come on baby, light my fire,' is blaring from the disco once again, and the Conga is halfway on its way to Treffin.

At a table near the bar Anthea, Ziggy's sister, is chain-smoking and indulging in a feminist rant. No way could she ever be a mother…

"I couldn't take all that shit," she says digging her elbow into the ribs of her sleepy-looking husband. As soon as she goes to the bar, he'll drop off. What's wrong with all these men falling asleep?

"He's not well," she says and then imitates a Treffin accent, as if she was above it all in her job at the Travel Agency. While she's there her thoughts are free to fly with the plane tickets to Rio and Morocco.

"Don't talk to me about a stag night; this pathetic specimen had a stag week, although you'd hardly think it, looking at him now."

A general cheer of "Oompah!" as her husband is photographed, too deeply submerged in his sleep to notice.

"Oh…do the Okey Cokey…that's what it's all about!"

It's the rather insignificant relatives from Llanelli who take centre stage. "Southwalians," as Uncle Norman refers to them rather dubiously. The husband, who hasn't a tooth in his head, dances full of youthful vigour and *joie de vivre* with his wife – 'That's what it's all about.' What does she see in him? thinks Auntie Edna. They dance the night away and are subject to several 'oompah' pictures and a great deal of attention, but nobody quite knows who they are. A couple of skeletons from the family cupboard perhaps?

"We don't speak much Welsh," says the husband and then in Welsh in a heart-warming southern dialect: "We speak a different Welsh, see. We say '*Be ti'n moyn?*' when we go to the bar, but you lot are real Northwalians."

Quiet Lynne, a real old sly boots, has her eye on the wedding cake before anyone else gets a chance to cut it. To such a degree that she fantasises about scraping the back with her nails without anyone noticing, and stuffing it all into her mouth. If she doesn't, it'll just mean that the staff of the Crossville Club will be gorging themselves on it after everyone's gone.

At the end of the evening comes the slow numbers and the slobbery kissing in the dark. An Oompah Party for the masses, and every flash and film forgotten in that last dance '*Save the Last Dance for Me.*' Everyone clinging together until the guests are released into the damp night air.

A week after the party and a chance to see the Great Oompah party photos, and the privilege of hearing from Auntie Hettie how it is you too are distantly related to the most boring man in the world!

Early at Service

I'd enjoy arriving early for a service at Capel y Graig and taking up my place in the cosy confines of the back row. From there I could observe the congregation. As motley a crew of characters as you'd find among Chaucer's pilgrims, as colourful as the hues of the Bayeux tapestry. Some entering so sheepishly through the door that they seemed to be almost apologetic for having the temerity to stray over the threshold. Others bustling in bold as brass ready to show off their latest finery, exhibiting the same pride as Siân Owen in her borrowed shawl in Vosper's famous painting.

At about a quarter to ten, the old guard would arrive, the elderly chapel members with their secure smiles, intent on getting a particular place among the new neutral seating, which to Daniel Owen's character, Wil Bryan, would probably seem like postage stamps. Their haste was not undignified, however, and their eagerness to get a good view did not prevent them from giving a welcoming wave and having a chat. At this juncture the organist would begin going through their paces as the main body began to flow in for ten o' clock.

By that time the car park would be jam packed with smart limousines and the Minister would be at the door, shaking hands with the faithful as they arrived. Several would manage to slip through the Minister's welcoming net. Some were obviously worthy of his special attention while others gained access unmolested. Perhaps some of the flock required less shepherding than others. The congregation would murmur expectantly, waiting to take their lead from the front, and some of the women would have already have spotted someone or something worthy of note. A young woman, perhaps, who had not been to chapel for ages, blushing at of all the attention she was attracting from those who actually remembered who she was; or a child, perhaps, calmly contemplating all and sundry and waving uninhibitedly at Uncle Fred.

Next to turn up would be Brian, who doesn't have much Welsh, and who tends to sit at the back – his conscience probably pricked after being cornered by the Minister at some coffee morning or other a few months ago.

Before long, the chapel elders would settle themselves in the front pew on either side of the pulpit, slipping into their seats in a suitably dignified manner, lending a heartfelt helping hand to the more infirm brethren. This month's announcer would shuffle his notes and practise his lines to himself.

"Holy, holy, holy, Lord God Almighty' – the opening refrain and the congregation raise their eyes to the pulpit. In the silence before that first hymn, Nerys would make a late appearance in the splendour of her new outfit and make-up thereby ensuring that her entrance would not go unnoticed. And she'd get the stares alright… Oh! Here she is again, the little show off! Others, however, would be more tolerant, accepting that Nerys is always late for everything and knowing her to be more of a Christian than half the congregation. She'd hold on tightly to the silver cross round her neck throughout the service. Next to her would be Jill, her grey hairs well disguised – lovely girl, although she's long lost her true authenticity like so many others in this world. At her side would sit her husband. He's no great believer for sure. Rather out of his depth he'd sit there

rather uncomfortably at times with a faraway look in his eyes. Behind them were Mr and Mrs Johnson. Salt of the earth. They'd been living in a little terraced cottage for years and would go off to relations in Folkstone for their annual holidays. Mr Johnson lived for his bowls after he retired and his wife was quite happy to lead a very simple life. But she was rather hurt when the Minister's wife sailed passed her one day without so much as a smile or wave. Things weren't as they used to be.

I remember one particular service – the first after the summer holidays it was. The opening hymn had gone well – as was usually the case with this particular service. Davida Davies was in love with her Casablanca hat. She sang like a linnet, enouncing every word with the utmost clarity and giving every sentence the full professional treatment. A television crew had filmed a service back in the spring and everyone had thought that the cameras had given Davida too much attention on that occasion. On that first Sunday in September, her little daughter stood obediently by her side, getting to look more and more like her mother every day. However, Davida was canny and insightful enough to realise that everything about her was a bit of an act, and she had to exercise a considerable degree of control at times to stop herself from bursting out laughing in the middle of her singing. Despite her primadonna antics, you could nevertheless sense the inherent diffidence of a country upbringing. Certainly she looked as though her thoughts were on the countryside.

The cortege around Miss West were giving it all they could that day, but the latter's singing was as abysmal as ever. Also she would always look incredibly suspicious of whatever message emanated from the pulpit. She didn't think the chapel was the right place to discuss politics. There had been quite enough of that during the 'Yes for Wales' campaign and Sunday Closing. Now, it was all about nuclear weapons. There was always some fashionable band-wagon to jump on.

Behind her Dyfed Morgan, a journalist with a national daily, was used to people of every type. He would read the hymn rather than actually sing it. He believed that the failings of present-day ministers lay in the demise of the magnificent old hymns and so he would simply stick to reading one verse in rather desultory tones. He stared at the CND badge adorning the scarf of a young girl in front of him. He didn't think that chapel members actually needed to join such movements. He sat down at the end of the hymn his head bowed reverently. For a man who worked in such a competitive and intrepid industry he looked so very small.

Huw Edwards prepared himself for the first reading from the pulpit. He came from the north of the county and was full of facts and anecdotes about old chapels and the revival. His wife sat beside him, a good-natured Welsh woman, but one who would often pretend that her Welsh was not as good as her husband's, just so she could show off her English and feel different. She sat swaddled in her fur coat behind her big glasses.

Carol wasn't getting anything from the reading and switched off the moment the Minister announced ... "The reading this morning comes from the third chapter of the Book of Proverbs" ... this gave her a chance to think about last night all through the reading... about Rob... his caresses as they danced to a George Michael number in the *Night Owl*, the slow dance in the dark shadows and then ... It was time for the second hymn and a chance for her to look round and take in the latest hairstyles, or a particularly interesting looking skirt. Why couldn't she get her hands on something like that?

Llinos stood up, winking at her children as they grappled with the hymn book and thumbed their way to the right page. Her eyes were full of goodness and theirs full of mischief. They sang for all they were worth and during the prayers they put their hands together in a most devout manner. It was easy to spot Robat Jones by the central aisle at the back, agreeing with every reading and hymn tune. He empathised with every nuance of the hymnists' words, revelling in the depths of their black night and the heavenly light provided by Christ for the lantern which lit their paths. He stared at the floor, his Simon Peter-like bulk responding to each and every syllable.

Owain came around with the collection to the rear of the chapel, a gospel-like radiance filling his features. In Owain's eyes Christ's torch burned as brightly now as it had in the beginning, like the first smile of the Resurrection. There too could be seen the searing penetration of the final nail of the Crucifixion. The anguish and the joy were a synergy within him and he still remembered the formative experiences of his teenage years when he first accepted God into his heart. The strength and purity of that innocence still remained fresh in everything he did.

Wil sang the children's hymn at the top of his voice, just as if he were in the rugby club after stop tap on Saturday night. He didn't have much of a singing voice, but he'd give it all he'd got, drowning out all the sweeter voices around him as he murdered each and every melody. Wil was of the opinion that the formality of the whole place should be given a bit of a shake-up to make it bit earthier, a bit more like the rugby club even. He felt the old stagers needed a bit of a kick in the right place. But did anyone listen to him?

The end of the children's hymn was always a turning point in the service, marking the end, as it were, of the family service. The children would flow like quicksilver into the schoolroom at the back for the Sunday School and a small army of devoted workers would slip out at the same time to offer guidance to the these bright little minds. The rest would stay for the sermon. The Minister from his 'gleaming pinnacle on high' assessing the hotchpotch of characters who remained.

And so another service came to an end. The congregation lingered on chatting in the doorway and the car park as the back-seat observer made his way home, his head full of vivid impressions, but the words of the text and the three headings of the sermon already forgotten.

The Christmas Pagan

It was a busy grey morning just before Christmas and mam and dad and the kids were out in force on Bangor High Street in the madcap rush to ensure the usual haul of presents required for a traditional family Christmas.

In front of Woolworths stood the local hospital radio station caravan, its festive celebrations providing a heart-warming antidote to the drudgery of shopping with balloons for the children and Shakin' *Merry Christmas Everyone* Stevens blasting out his Christmas anthem. The tireless efforts of the balloon blowers created a real party atmosphere, although there were very few who paused to consider exactly whose birthday was being celebrated.

A café provides a welcome refuge from the hordes of shoppers and a chance for me to sit down. There's only one empty table, although there is obviously someone else sitting opposite to me, their coat is draped over the back of the chair which is besieged by a cluster of bags and presents. "Someone's been busy," I say to myself, "and they're taking a bit of a risk too leaving their things like this."

The owner of the coat and shopping returned to the table, a young guy about thirty with flame-red hair and a face etched with life experience. He engaged me in conversation straight away, locating my dialect as being from the Bala area and launching into all the family connections he had in that part of Wales.

My order arrived – a baked potato, cheese, onion and *chilli con carne*.

"Don't you eat meat then?" enquired my fellow diner.

"Not very often, but I can't really say I'm a vegetarian, although I could become one quite easily."

"I've given up drinking, and pretty well stopped smoking, but I don't think I could give up eating meat."

He then went on to talk about his experiences following his heavy drinking and how things had got out of hand.

'I remember waking up in the back garden or France… or Ireland, and realising that it was actually a problem. I just couldn't stop. It was impossible for me to stop after just a couple. I'd have to take it to the very edge. But I feel that I've got better control of it now. People are my drug now. People wherever I go. And travel, that's the other great pleasure. I have to travel. Usually, people of my age have settled down with a wife and mortgage. But a car's more important to me… so I can escape…"

Bangor and its shops were now far from my mind as I journeyed along with his memories.

"Why don't you write your memoirs?"

"It's all up here," he pointed to his head. "A lot of it would be X-certificate anyway."

"That doesn't matter, if you tell the truth. There isn't enough stuff in Welsh which tells the truth."

"Things that Nain would not approve of. Chatting with a whore in an Amsterdam pub. She'd a perfectly good job before that, but then she turned to the red lights to make more money."

"Was she a sad person?"

"I don't think she was sad. She was bright enough, and she'd be out every night in the pub, with her friends. Just like me. All the travelling I do changes your attitude to things. I don't have any prejudices now against people of other nations. How can I judge Americans by just meeting one of them on their holidays in Wales? And friends – some of them are gay – well, I can't judge them. It's not my place to judge them. I'm much more open since I've been travelling and the so-called big problems we have in this country seem like nothing when you get back. I escape by going off into the mountains or into the world of sports now. Things are more organised, more under control."

"Do you teach?" I asked. What a revealing question!

"No, I look after disadvantaged children. I've just been for a month's holiday with them to Ireland. It was really important that one lad, who was dying from cancer, enjoyed himself on the trip. I was sharing a room with him and one morning he woke up and decided to make me a cup of coffee – using half the tin to do so. There was coffee everywhere, up the walls. Everywhere. But he was really enjoying himself."

He paused momentarily and finished his tea before returning to his recollections.

"I remember another time when we were in Ireland… the trouble is, you see, I'm too soft. We went there for three days and we saw a mother and her child begging on the street and another child, about fifteen years of age, sleeping rough on one of the bridges over the Liffey."

For a few brief moments I was aware of the sound of the shoppers all around us and their Christmas cheer and bonhomie.

"People here in Bangor don't know about that sort of poverty," the red-haired man continued. "I booked the lad into a hostel and he got a chance to wash and rest, and I'd got fifty quid left over and I could have stayed on for another couple of days quite comfortably. But I didn't. I couldn't carry on enjoying myself after seeing that. So I said to him, "Go on take it." I don't know what he spent the money on, but at least I had given it to him."

This man's beautiful vision of the world was of a series

of villages where all people were brothers and sisters.

"That was a very Christian thing to do," I said.

"I'm not religious either. I'm a pagan. A pagan. Particularly after some of the experiences I've had – sexually, I mean. I know a good title for a book of my memoirs – *Gutters of Europe*."

On the surface I was a bit shocked. But I couldn't help but think of Cynan's lines in the *Ballad of the Four Kings*.

> *And just as much as you did to these,*
> *You did to the Lord of the pure driven snow.*

But I wasn't really present in the café by that time; I'd slipped into a fanciful Utopia rather than facing up to reality.

"So what do you call it then if it isn't Christianity – good deeds?" I suggested. There was a silence.

"I remember once I was travelling in Denmark and asking in Danish for somewhere to stay and this Scottish guy looking at me in disbelief. "Aye, an' could you say that again in English, please?" He was a night club owner and I got to stay at his place that evening. He warned me not to go to some places in the city – in Copenhagen – and of course the first thing I did the very next day was to go to those places. I remember going to a pub near the docks. It was full of some really hard cases. About this time of year it was, and after they'd found out that I was Welsh and that Wales was different from England, they wanted me to sing. Well, after I'd worked my way through the repertoire I sang 'Silent Night' in Welsh and the whole pub joined in their languages."

So this was the Great Christmas Pagan!

It was time for him to gather his bags and be on his way to get ready for work that evening. I felt that there wasn't really any point in urging him again to write about his experiences. I was content just to have been one of those people from the four corners of the globe who had experienced his affable nature over the course of a meal in a café and perhaps he would count me as being among his host of friends.

"It's been great meeting you. Best of luck now."

I sat there with snatches of our conversation still bouncing off the walls of my brain, unlocking old dreams and making me realise that there are still good people left in the world. This café certainly seemed to attract such people.

After a few minutes I got up and went to pay at the till.

"It's been paid," said the girl. I stared at her open-mouthed.

"The guy who was sitting with you... he's paid for you."

Dean and Debs

Dean's Soliloquy 1

However much I kid myself, even the video and the satellite aren't really much company after a while. Neither are the beer cans, although there's no shortage of those either. I was just leaving the house with a couple of tins when an old school friend came by – the only person who calls apart from Mam, fair play to her. Perhaps she feels she has to after I found out about everything. She's good to me, mind. Brings my washing and tells me I should tidy the place up a bit – and that I should get more than one chair now that Deb's gone. Mam keeps the place tidy. The three piece suite went and I lost Debs with the job.

Not that I really blame the buses. I'm happy enough driving a bus but there's too many temptations. Mostly school girls who say 'hiya' and smile all silly like, and occasionally someone like Alison.

Alison was special; I met her on the bus. A nice girl working in the wardrobe department in Chester Theatre. She had a bit of gipsy in her. I lived with Ali in Hope. Live in Hope and die in Caergwrle, as they say, and get buried in Cefn-y-bedd! She had a bungalow there – I got my meals for free, everythin', and she'd changed her car insurance so that I could drive too.

Yeah, that's where I was when my friend called and couldn't get an answer. I was there for about three weeks, living with Ali. That's why there was no lights on in the house and why the curtains hadn't been opened for a while. Nothing's safe round here.

But she wanted more from the relationship than I did – and I wanted to be free. I didn't want to be trapped. But I didn't talk to her about it, I just walked out. There's too much temptation at work, right enough – that's why Debs went. But perhaps she needed her freedom too? I'd known her since I was fifteen and I've heard from the latest reports in the pub – I go to nightclubs too – that she's made up for everything she's lost now. She wants to join the Navy and she's going with some bloke who's in the Navy. I'm still friends with Alison too – don't misunderstand me – and I go drinking in Caergwrle on Saturday night, and I'll phone her to ask if she wants to come out for a drink. Just for a drink. To pay for a drink.

I think I'll be giving up this bus-driving lark – some of the people you meet are OK, but keeping to the timetable and putting up with the abuse you get from the passengers is somethin' else. I've been offered work part-time behind the bar in the *Seven Stars*. They know me now I'm drinking round town again. Nice people there, but I'm not sure. And I'm friends with the manageress of Benetton – not that we went out or anything. She's black and she asked if I'd model clothes for her of an evening for a fashion show. I must pop in tomorrow to tell her I'm game. I haven't got the body for it really, but I'm dyeing my hair lighter and I've asked my brother to get some razor blades from school to keep the back like the barber does it. It's starting to turn ginger as the roots grow out. In the new job, if my hair was still brown – it would have turned grey by now!

Dean's Soliloquy – November

Brrr! The winter's here already and I decided that as it was the first of November I'd put up the Christmas decorations. Make Christmas last a long time.

Debs is back with me. It's been a month now – she's moved back in completely today. Can't live without me. It's nice having her stuff around, particularly after the break-in. I've forgotten about it now to be honest, but as Debs would say. 'It would have to happen to me!' They stole the lot – the CD player, the video and left a hell of a mess. Somehow, they managed to shut the backdoor again, and I hadn't noticed. But they kicked it down to start with.

They've moved out from next door and the council came and boarded up the place after someone chucked a brick through the window. Nothing's safe round here once they know you've got something new. Debs' things are back now, making the place feel cosy. I can't tell you how happy I am to see things like her undies back drying on the heater. Perhaps she just feels sorry for me. She's the only one who does. She's a better friend than Craig was – I don't have anything to do with him now because he knows who's got my stuff. School friend or not, I won't trust him again. It always happens to me.

Debs came home this afternoon saying that she's filling in for her sister's job in the knicker factory – two days a week. Debs isn't so sure about the Navy now, if she can get good work round here. I'm still busy on the buses – going past my old school really slowly and giving a wave in case I see my brother, or else going dead fast if I see some of the old teachers!

I've stopped drinking a lot now – I only drink at home. Saving money. I'm still paying for the CD-player and the video which got nicked. Debs is bringing her television and stereo and, 'cos the thieves didn't take the satellite,

I'm quite happy to watch *Pretty Woman* again tonight. I was watching *Rambo* this afternoon – I've seen it twice before and it's not quite as good as the others 'cos he's fightin' the Russians all on his own at the end. What an absolute load of shite.

My brother, Dyfed's broken the bone in his big toe playing football, so he won't be at school for the cross-country for Children In Need on Friday. I'll have to watch how I drive on Friday morning in case I knock one of them down. I hated cross-country at school. I was always last and too fat. I'm a bit different now – more like Jason Donovan.

I try to be really cool – and look how people are so ready to swallow things. Take Alison for instance, Live in Hope? No bloody Hope. I've got power in my hands now, I'm not ugly, I'm really chic. I'm starting to enjoy believing in this and I'm thinking about myself for once.

Winter's on its way and my lonely little Christmas tree is taking its stand against y Wern at the moment. I hope no one steals the satellite.

Dean's Soliloquy 3 – Advent

Another really gloomy evening. Nothing on the satellite tonight, just some film which made Debs cry with that dancer – Patrick Swayze. I could move like him if I had his money. *Ghost* it was called, and she was saying things like "Oh, Dean, it's so sad they can't be together." But I'm not going to take any notice of her. I bought her the soundtrack to *Dirty Dancing* about a month back to shut her up. She likes the song *We had the time of our lives*. I don't think much of it myself. I had a bit of money to spare to buy the CD because I'm helping a friend of a friend to take fruit and veg round QP – on the side like. I'm working the taxis now for a while over Christmas.

Plenty of demand at this time of year. I was glad to finish on the buses. You can please yourself a bit more with a taxi, just so long as you treat the girls in the office OK.

There's a few satellites in the street now, but my dish was the first. I'm a bit sleepy tonight and I haven't changed out of my leather trousers, silk shirt and braces or taken the earrings off. You have to dress smart – tart yourself up for the taxi. You get to know some of the customers. Some better than others.

It's hard work, but a least I don't have to drive that bloody bus up to Brynglawdd. The blonde highlights in my hair are on the way out and the roots are brown again. Well, brownish. Debbie can't do the colour for me tonight because she's flat out on the settee. She didn't cook supper for me either. I've been working all day and she's been lying there with the gas fire on full blast. She's throwing up every morning. The doctor's been here to see her today, and she's got bronchitis. She's got to take antibiotics and she's swallowing them down with red Corona – my bottle too! The doctor asked her whether she was expecting, 'cos if she was, some sorts of tablets would be bad for her. Well, as she said 'you can't be sure – you can never be sure, can you?' Well, these days! So, she went and got some other tablets, just in case. But she must have told Denise, her best friend, because her boyfriend sees me in the Offy and asks "How do you feel? Now you're goin' to be a dad? Are you looking forward to it." And I just go "Well, alright … Yeah… alright."

I heard her telling Denise that I appreciate her more now, since she came back to me. I don't know why she told her. She's a real little vixen and I hate having her in the house. But at least if that's what she thinks!

I've got a new car and I park by the house in case someone tries to nick it. Seventy quid it cost me from the dad of one of the bus drivers from Abermorddu. At least it moves! I only use it for going to and from work at the moment. All the way to the taxi rank in King Street. Well, it's better than walking. Isn't it?

Debs is talking about getting married, but I'm not. I don't talk about it to anyone anyway. I'm a very private like that. But she insists on bringing it up in front of other people. I just change the subject. And she brings all her giggly friends round and friggin Denise cluckin' away like some big fat hen in the middle of 'em, and they'll all talk about Weddings. "You take the high road and I'll take the low road," and give them the finger. "Swivel on that."

Oh, bloody hell, someone's knockin' at the window! I know. It'll be Mam wanting her lino laid and I've just settled down to relax. Oh well, I can't avoid Mam! She gives Debs a kiss and says she's looking better. She'd even look better walking down the aisle in white on my arm than she does now – all curled up in a big sweaty lump on the settee.

Deb's Soliloquy – Christmas

Dean and me's been going out together since I was fifteen. He dressed different and used make-up at that time. That was the attraction – he was different. But he was trying to come to terms with who his dad was. I know we've gone through a lot the last three years and that I'm going to be eighteen tomorrow and I'm pregnant with his child, but, honest to God, that's all I want in life. I'm well used to seeing my sisters with their kids and I'm relaxed around them, and I'm going to enjoy being a mam. I'm happy living round by here too 'cos this is my patch. They all know me round here – I'm one of the girls who was brought up in the shadow of the Power House, and they can remember me as being a really bad lot at school, and that I used to give the Pakis at the chip shop a fair bit of stick. I'd go in sometimes and ask for fresh hot chips, not the old ones that's been sitting around in the fryer for half an hour. "And if I don't get them I'll tell everyone in the queue that you're sellin' yesterday's chips". But they all used to laugh and take it OK from me.

I was really ill yesterday, and stayed in bed all day. At six in the evening I'd finished all my fags and Dean wouldn't go for me – so there was nothing for it but to put on me coat and walk down to the Paki shop in me slippers. I made some joke about getting more chocolate coloured make-up and they all laughed.

Don't get me wrong about school – I'm not thick. I just didn't work hard enough. But nobody can run rings round me. Now Dean's working late on the taxis, I'm on my own then. I prefer watching a film on the satellite than going to sleep before he gets home – or the old video of *Ghost*. I always have to get the Kleenex ready for that one. Dean really likes it too.

I've been getting ready for the baby for ages, since I lost my job. I've been collecting different things for him… or her. Although I've seen the scan, I've asked them not to tell me what it's going to be or all the magic will go out of it. I was worried that I wasn't very big but now things are OK. I've been on that machine too, the one which tells you if your baby's scared and things like that. All this technology's fantastic, but not half as fantastic as the birth itself.

"Debs, can we have a word with you in the office, love?" That's how things ended at the knicker factory and after my being so loyal and everythin' to them and there was talk that I might be made supervisor of our department in the new year. But they heard that I was pregnant, and it was easier for them to sack me for faulty work in order to avoid paying for my maternity. Well, I told them: "You've shit on me." That's the only sort of language they understand. "I don't want any of your money.

And my eyes were filling up and not one of them offered me as much as a cup of tea or a handkerchief. They just left me standing there. And they'd all been calling me Debs and saying 'hiya' to me every morning.

It was something of a blessing in disguise as it happens, 'cos I've got something more now. And Dean's attitude's changed. He's grown up and since we've got back together he's a different person. He's promised to look for more permanent work in the new year, and I'm going to help him live his dream – of going into the police or becoming a prison officer. Lift him above the world of taxis. There's so much can go wrong with the engine – he doesn't get fair play.

I'm the only one who knows him – the only one who's gone to the trouble of getting to know him. I know we went our different ways for a short while – It was during this time that Dean changed and lost weight, and went all trendy. Not the Dean I knew at all. He bought flowers for someone else on the buses and not for me. It was just the once.

All his problems come from when he was fat as a young lad because for a while he wanted to be Jason Donovan – he had to prove that to himself. He dyed his hair blonde, he'd got two earrings and a gold watch to attract the girls on the buses. He lost about a stone and a half because there was no food in the house. But for him losing weight was just a boost to his ego.

The old Dean returned thank goodness, and I said goodbye to Gaz who was going into the Navy anyway. A temporary thing. I can relax during the day now although I'm trying to do some tidying up and painting, and trying to get the little room ready for the baby.

I told Dean when he was rather quiet the other evening: "Don't you worry that I lost the job. When I'm twenty-one, we'll all go on a wonderful holiday, 'cos I can get to me money when I'm twenty-one."

Dean went to the factory, fair play to him, to see the manager about the way they treated me. And do you know what? The manager was hiding behind the door; he didn't want to meet Dean.

"Don't get your knickers in a twist," he says. What a stupid thing to say in a knicker factory! I'd have loved to have been a fly on the wall. Oh, well, it's all over now, and Dean's getting some money on the taxis to keep the three of us.

Aye, I've got something better than all of them.

A Thousand Times More Beautiful ...

Sweet child of mine, *hei lwli lwli*
Just, close your eyes now, little baby
I'm beginning to tire of rocking you gently
So just go to sleep, my pretty child, go to sleep *hei lwli*

I love Elfyn and the whole world's turned to summer. But nobody knows that I love Elfyn because I'm not supposed to. It's only you who knows, my sweet little baby. Mammy's not supposed to love anyone except Daddy, is she, babes? No, she certainly isn't. But Mammy does love Daddy sometimes, when she can get his attention. Before he goes off guzzling pints every night.

Daylight fades within these walls
The candles flicker as darkness falls,
Play is ended but never fear,
'Cos Daddy comes home as night draws near.

We like that, don't we, babes? Mammy loves Uncle Elfyn and you're going to get to know Uncle Elfyn really well because I'm going to make sure that he's going to be a godfather to you. Then I can be with him formally, officially, so that no one will suspect anything for ever and ever amen. Naughty Mammy sees Uncle Elfyn in chapel. That's why she goes there and everything looks respectable.

To me Elfyn's smiles are much more valuable
Than all the gold in the world
And the rocking of your cradle ...

What a naughty Mammy you've got, changing the words of your lullaby like that.

*   *   *

Hello, babes. Mammy's been a real old sly puss. She's been talking to Auntie Carys and trying to look interested in her life, in order to find out more about *him*. I'll milk her of every last drop, 'cos she's too friendly with him. I won't hold back, I won't give up. Mammy's not one to do that. Mammy's going to invite Uncle Elfyn over to see us both and to love us. He'll be here before long. Naughty Mammy hasn't phoned so much recently because he's starting to get twitchy, starting to play funny games and not give Mammy… or you, of course, my beautiful little girl… as much attention.

I'd like to have him here in the house right now, with Daddy a long way away and you fast asleep and…

> To bed, to bed, all children get to bed,
> To bed, to bed, all children get to bed.

Do you think, sugar candy, that Uncle Elfyn would take pity on us both and let us live with him? He's got plenty of room. He showed me round when I called past. He thinks that I'm just a friend. Things haven't been too good with his family's health recently – and so enter big, bad Mammy with cakes and brimming with concern, so she can make enquiries and get even nearer. Get closer and take possession of him..

> Trot trot trot ride the white mare,
> Trot trot trot all the way to the fair,
> Trot trot trot, what do we see?
> Mammy coming home with something nice for tea.

*   *   *

Mammy's expecting again. Who's the father this time, I wonder? Actually, I know it's Brian. So it won't just be you and me around the place before too long, sugar dumpling. We'd better get you baptised pretty soon and get Uncle Elfyn as your godfather. All my stories of losing one baby after another didn't have any effect this time, or the one about my Uncle in Brecon dying suddenly, or that Dad wasn't my real dad, and that I was adopted.

A year ago, when Uncle Elfyn came to the house to welcome Brian and me to our new home – to our new neighbourhood – and Brian wasn't here of course, I asked him to push the pram – your pram, babes. We went shopping to the village just like a family. He didn't like the picture, he was uneasy, and I liked the picture so much. I took several. I'm still reliving the whole thing. I just can't delete it. He's mine and I want to offer you, the fruit of my womb, to him. I'll have to pull myself together now because I can hear Daddy's car in the drive. Time for an English rhyme, I think, with Daddy around.

> Rock-a-bye baby on the tree top
> When the wind blows
> The cradle will rock.
> When the bow breaks
> The cradle will fall…

*   *   *

Uncle Elfyn wasn't in chapel. I bet you he's been at some wild all-night parties somewhere with someone. He's forgotten about Seion. The bugger. He's too tricky by half… a bit like you are sometimes, *cariad bach*.

Uncle Elfyn would take Mammy to Welsh things. He'd give me some attention, take me to chapel and out for meals and to Theatr Clwyd. That's the sort of life he's got and that would suit my image nicely. I need to be respectable. At the christening, when Uncle Elfyn becomes a godfather, I'll have to arrange a little buffet in the village hall and I'll have to be the mistress of ceremonies, as it were. I want them at home to see once and for all that this daughter too can do something just as well as the rest of her siblings, who never come to see her here, but who do everything just right.

We will rock you, rock you, rock you very patiently until that day dawns..

*   *   *

Lies are useful things, *cariad bach*, just so long as I remember when I'm telling them! I've been telling them to Uncle Elfyn since I've known him, but he thinks very highly of me. I've told him that I've made radio programmes, and that I nursed Hywel Gwynfryn in Penarth Hospital. I've told so many lies to people, sometimes I'm not sure what the truth is – holidays in Paris, a little illness in Llandudno Hospital, a car accident, you having fits, my little chick – anything to get to Uncle Elfyn once and for all... to have and to hold, isn't it?

I wonder whether Uncle Elfyn will be at the new minister's inauguration meeting tonight? I want to phone in case I have a wasted journey and if he answers I'm going to pretend I've phoned the wrong number.

Then, I'll wear my tight jeans so he can see how much weight I've lost. All a naïve young girl like me wants to do is chat, isn't it? Big bad Mammy is going to smile at him in the inauguration meeting during the hymn:

> Who shall tell of this love?
> So inscrutable is the Lord above.

Oooh – yeah. Here's a love like the deepest ocean, as the hymn says. I won't let him go without a fight.

*   *   *

Mammy's sent a note. I think I've paid a high price for my mistakes. The time has come to put the past behind me – there we are. I wonder how that went down at nine o' clock on a wet Saturday morning.

Gee up little horsey carrying you and me
A-gathering nuts the other side of the Dee;
There's water in the river and the rocks are very slick
We both fall in together. Well, what a dirty trick.

*   *   *

You don't listen to your old mam, do you? Why not? What did I ever do to you? It doesn't matter how many years it takes for our relationship to get back on the rails. I can't wait for Uncle Elfyn but he doesn't get to punish you by not being a godfather, he doesn't get to hurt you. Shame on him for refusing!

In the inaugural meeting, my little dove, you could see the colours of his new jumper from Top Man really glowing and you kept reaching out to touch it. I knew what you wanted but naughty old uncle turned away.

I'm wrapping Elfyn in chains, and the only way he can break free is if he rumbles my little subterfuge.

I nursed my sweet boy child
On my breast and watched him grow,
Deio, you were that child
And where you are now I do not know;
It's so long since last I saw you,
My darling child, are you well?
If you can't get to see me, sweet Deio,
Just send a letter, your news to tell.

I don't want to give you a chance to behave like Deio, my beautiful baby doll.

Cleansed

What was she doing in a strange man's bath in Swindon? What was she doing amongst all this Body Shop stuff? Wearing the scent of a totally different woman, she was now worried that someone would notice that she had been pilfering among their lotions and potions when they got home.

Why was she there? This was the question that kept coming back to her as she soaped herself in the foaming white bubbles of this enormous and totally unfamiliar bath? She wasn't sure how she'd actually got there – into the bath, that is. Somehow she'd managed to ask despite her fluttering nerves and Geoff had said: "You're welcome to have a bath."

She had got to know Geoff over the phone. She'd never seen him until today at the Swindon hospital radio studio, but, over the past months, their telephone friendship had become increasingly intense.

It had all started when Swindon Hospital Radio phoned up the Hospital Radio in Treffin to enquire about the most popular records played over the airwaves for some survey or other. Since then, every Thursday evening without fail, Laura would get a phone call from this guy in Swindon. She would joke about her "man in Swindon" with her young associates at the studio, but she said nothing to her husband about him.

Laura began to look forward to Geoff's calls, to rely on

them, not that there was anything untoward about them in terms of their content – they would simply chat about the weather, music and each other's families.

They had met on the phone, and yet now, somehow or other here she was in his bath with his wife far from home with their child, on holiday visiting Nana in Barnsley. Laura added a little more hot water to the tub. She might as well enjoy the facilities after such a long journey.

Laura was on her way to visit another hospital radio and to stay with her old school friend, Sarah, in London. That was the official version for her husband's benefit, Ralph, and he hadn't tried to stop her.

Her husband, Ralph, was a labourer who earned his living from fencing or building work – a hard graft which left him exhausted and filthy dirty at the end of each and every working day. He would go off to bed early before *Coronation Street*, leaving Laura to her own lotions and potions and loneliness in the company of the cat.

Thursday evening gave her a break from this incarcerating routine, when she did her stint as a volunteer at the hospital radio, introducing a programme of middle-of-the-road music with the occasional surprise thrown in to keep everyone on their toes in their beds as it were, and to show that she was still alive – *Simply the Best* from Tina Turner suddenly blasting out somewhere between Mantovani and Trebor Edwards.

She'd become so middle-of-the-road herself, and she was desperate for a bit of a change. She wanted to do something unexpected. Something rash even. Hence her present location… if Ralph suspected for one moment…

She smiled as she reflected on her situation. She examined her body under the water, below the shrinking soapy islands on the surface. *Islands in the Stream* by Kenny Rogers and Dolly Parton came to mind – one of her listeners' favourites. Suddenly she had an overwhelming urge to burst out in uncontrollable laughter right in the middle of this strange bathroom.

The urge ebbed away as she realised she would soon have to get out of the suds and go down stairs to face the music with Geoff...

After a rapid express train journey from Chester, she had made a whistle-stop tour round the hospital radio at Swindon General. Up to that point her actions had been totally transparent and fully sanctioned by an unsuspecting Ralph.

Her journey from there to the large house in the suburbs remained cloaked in secrecy however, concealed by the encroaching darkness creeping over the town. She saw no signs of the neighbours. Everyone was safely ensconced in their little boxes. She was afraid of making too much noise as she pulled the plug on her bath in case next door suspected something.

But nobody seemed to have their noses in your business round here, so very different from her own neighbours at home, and the closely guarded secrets of her own family.

Here she had seemingly been able to slip into the house with its drawn curtains as unnoticed as a shadow.

Tugging the plug, she rose from the soapy waters.

She didn't know what Geoff's expectations might be as he waited downstairs. She didn't know what she expected of Geoff. But she felt as if she could well be sharing his bed that evening – an evening free from her husband – if that's what she wanted.

It was all so close now.

Geoff had often gone on about his marriage and his kids on the phone over the last few months and Laura felt as if she knew the whole family quite well. She would like to have children, she mused as she wrapped herself in the luxurious bath sheet neatly folded over the heated towel rail.

She was glad that she had taken the step, that she had broken away from the fetters and wrenched herself out of the monotonous rut of life with Ralph and the late night phone calls with friends from the radio studio long after her spouse had gone off to bed.

What had happened to the kindness the flowers and the fun they had enjoyed in the early stages of the relationship? It had all disappeared under a pile of cans and TV suppers while she squirmed miserably, her face to the wall in sheer frustration, trapped in a silent prison the thought of which set her stomach churning.

She felt a certain guilt that she had had to travel as far as Swindon to make her protest. But she just had to meet the voice on the phone. She felt that once Geoff had seen her, the idea of romance would fade, but...

While she was in the bath she remembered the words of another of her co-presenters at the cosy studio with its view towards the moor. Another man as it happened. Somehow she seemed to enjoy a better relationship with men – they weren't as bitchy, they weren't like the sly snakes she had known among her female acquaintances. This particular man had warned her how people believed in the potential happiness of the grass that is greener, but that she could in fact adapt what she had already.

As she dried off the Body Shop soap bubbles from between her toes, she thought about Geoff. His wife was obviously a good and considerate woman, and perhaps all marriages went through these rocky patches. But she had to come here to the bath in Swindon, outside her familiar surroundings to see things objectively.

That was the problem with their lives in both Bangor-on-Dee and Swindon. Ruts. Ralph wasn't so bad that she couldn't actually stand him, nor was Geoff's wife for that matter. It was circumstances which had changed them, if they had changed at all. However, Laura insisted on change, on playing *Meatloaf* in the middle of James

Last and Richard Clayderman. At times she just had to avoid the middle-of-the-road.

The words of her quirky friend, Rosie from the restaurant in the Arcade, came to mind: "If you just set your sights on Mr Perfect, it's not going to be enough, because you'll never get to meet Mr A Little Below the Angels, Mr OK and Mr Quite Nice on your journey through life."

Laura half-smiled into the steamy mirror, but she had already decided.

She felt cleansed, more cleansed than she had felt for a long time, and the next day after a night in a single bed and a suitably civilised breakfast, Laura warned Geoff never to contact her again.

And her early morning departure in the taxi was as stealthy as her arrival.

Reaching the Note

A quiet crescent on a council estate is hardly where you'd expect to meet someone who had been at the Garden. The rather dilapidated row of prefabs was not really the location for someone familiar with the flamboyant costumes and greasepaint associated with Covent Garden.

A reporter from the local paper was on her way to interview Gwyn about his musical career and his years at the Garden, and also about how he had carried on singing until very recently. He would sing at concerts – classical music and oratorio in an entrancing baritone, but he was also a star at the local Snooker Club, a mere stone's throw from his present abode where he had found sanctuary with a certain Mrs Roberts – a woman who understood him. One of the few who ever did so. Agnes Roberts was an elderly widow who had taken an old rebel under her wing.

However, it was now a rare event for Gwyn to sing at the Club, except at Christmas or Easter or on St David's Day – just to remind the buggers that they were in Wales. But there was a time and place for everything.

He'd spent the entire morning fumbling around through old drawers looking for the tape. *The* tape. Even Mrs Roberts had got down on her poor arthritic knees to assist in the search.

"I've found it, Agnes. Here it is." And after all his

exertions he flopped down exhausted with the sweat pouring from him.

He didn't manage to eat his lunch either and he waited for the ring at the door as if this interview were the most important of his entire life. Crikey, it was only some slip of a girl barely out of her nappies from the local rag. At one time, when he was at the Garden and acquainted with Sir Geraint, he'd be dealing with the best Fleet Street could throw at him! The Garden and its residents now seemed a long way off.

He heard a rustling behind the pale yellow curtains which shaded the room from the bright sunshine on the street outside. Gwyn put on his dark glasses and struggled to his feet.

This was to be one of Carys Puw's first assignments with the *Marcher Echo*. She had been sent by her boss to interview his old singing teacher. To provide Carys with some background material, the editor had brought into the office a picture of Gwyn in robust health together with an LP of his former talents.

As with most people on the border, neither the editor nor the singer came originally from the area, but from that other place beyond the hills where they were *proper Welsh*, as they'd say in the Club.

At every concert, Gwyn would try to sing Dafydd y Garreg Wen to remind himself of his roots, of that distant link. He would never forget Y Garreg Wen, and it was in the vicinity of the famous white rock immortalised by the renowned 18th century harpist, Dafydd Owen, that he desired for his ashes to be scattered when the time came.

The door was ajar but Carys rang the bell. Gwyn made his way into the hallway, his opening speech well rehearsed, 'Oh, it's open. Come on in.' He knew his lines, just as he'd known them at the Garden. Carys was unable to conceal her shock as she came face to face with this thin, jaundiced and sweaty looking individual with dark glasses which hid the paleness of his eyes. He bore no resemblance to the picture on the record sleeve, or the flattering portrait on the concert programme of several years ago.

"Come in. Tea? Coffee?" and the kettle immediately began to boil, Mrs Roberts remaining concealed somewhere in the background.

They talked of the usual things, the connection with her Editor, the Garreg Wen story, the influences of the Garden. But nothing was said of the present. That would be too cruel somehow.

"And these days I go down to see the troops at the Club. There aren't many who are Welsh there, mind, but they're a good bunch. I'll have a coffee with them – something stronger sometimes," He gazed at her redolently, smiling in a rather tragic playful manner from behind the dark glasses and revealing his yellow teeth. It was an uncontrollable smile and it was obvious that Carys was no great drinker or else she would have known the signs.

"Mrs Roberts looks after me... but I want you to listen to this tape. It's quite a recent one, St David's Day in the Leisure Centre with all the local male voice choirs. On this one I'm singing the *Dymestl – The Tempest* – with a really fantastic softening of the tone right at the end. Just listen to this – I hit a top 'G' on this."

And having started the tape in the dusty little cassette player, Gwyn sank back wearily into his seat, a glimmer of the old glory flashing somewhere behind the dark lenses. Sweating profusely and in some considerable pain, he mimed the familiar words. They listened intently together. Carys completely forgot where she was. The barking dogs and the cries of children on their summer holidays out in the street drifted away into the background.

The performance seemed to reflect his own

tempestuous life after the Garden, his voice swelling and softening before reaching an impressive grand finale. That afternoon, In the comfort of the room which was his haven from a world which had so badly hurt him, Gwyn seemed to come alive again.

A week later Carys was typing a tribute to him following his funeral near his beloved Garreg Wen. As she typed she felt glad that Gwyn had reached the note just one more time.

Bridge Building

Ali

Gareth came home over Christmas – three weeks leave, but he was scared they'd call him back again. He told me last time: 'Please, Mam, if the police come to get me, don't tell 'em where I am. I don't want to go to the Gulf."

Listen, Gareth," I tells him, 'I'm not goin' to tell a lie about you – I'm goin' to say where you are.'

'I'm not goin' to no soddin' Gulf,' he says and storms out of the house.

Anyway he thinks he's safe for a while 'cos they've moved all the Arctic training gear from Catterick down to Southampton and they're goin' off to Norway for their trainin' like they expected. He was supposed to go to Turkey too, before the balloon went up again. All this preparation costs absolute millions and two of his best mates have been sent there. After he heard from them he apologised to me.

"Sorry I told you not to say where I was," he says. "I feel terrible that I'm not out there with my friends." He got pictures of his friends in the post, and they're billeted in these really swish flats, and one of 'em was swimmin' in the sea just like he was on Barmouth beach, except they hadn't a stitch on 'em. I don't think he's so worried about being sent to the Gulf now. There were nice snaps of the apartment too and the lads having a laugh. But he's goin' off to Norway to start with – thank goodness.

It's a funny thing, but Gareth showed me a picture of himself this time and he was holdin' a gun.

"What are you doin' holdin' a gun?" I asks, and then I realised what a stupid question it was.

"We're always 'oldin' guns, Mam."

It was enough of a shock for me when he showed me a picture of himself in his battledress. I saw him on parade after six months – I went to Catterick to see that and he was wearin' a jumper an' trousers an' a baseball cap, and somehow I thought that's how it was goin' to be. And then, he shows me this picture of himself lyin' down and aimin' at a target, and I thought, 'our lad isn't supposed to play with guns.' And then I felt stupid 'cos that's what they're trained for, isn't it?

The *Cambrian News* have asked for a picture of everyone who's off to the Gulf, anyone who comes from along the coast here. I'm not sure Gareth would like that – having his picture in the paper and so on. He doesn't like attention.

Gareth's colour blind, see, so he can't be with the engineers, and he can't join the police – only if he goes on the wireless side of things. That's what he's doin' now. But when Gareth joined the army two years ago there was no mention of any more trouble in the Gulf – it's all blown up so quickly.

His trainin' was hard enough.

Part of it was havin' to be with a rabbit for a weekend camp. He had to get to know it and feed it an' look after it. Then as part of the exercise he had to kill it and cook it. Well, that story really turned my stomach. He refused to talk about some of the other things, and he was walkin' in his sleep – something he'd never done before. I think it'll be six years before he can come out. He signed up until then, and anyway he said he'd feel like a coward if he came out now. "Chicken," he called it. The idea of lettin' the lads down.

It was nice having Gareth and Cari at home over Christmas. They argue like any brother and sister, but it was nice havin' 'em round the house. Christmas Eve, I was drinkin' at work from about two in the afternoon – punch with all sorts of vodka in it an' then I went with Cari to the Last Inn.

"Come 'n 'ave a quick one with me," she goes. A quick one?! I didn't get out of there until seven! They were goin' down a treat, I'm tellin' you. I must have had ten vodkas, Then I went home and Jen and Adrian came down and stayed until ten and I was OK while they were there. But then they left and Gareth and Cari went off down to the snooker club, and while they were there I filled up a Christmas Stocking for each of 'em like I do every year. I've still done a stocking since the divorce, as best I can like. I had fun trying to pack the presents, as you can imagine! By eleven o' clock I'd got a splitting headache and I didn't feel too well. So I propped up the pillows good an' high in case I was sick and had a sort of a sleep.

Gareth and Cai got back around three in the morning and I woke up and I was feeling fantastic, and I was up then for a good while, cuddlin' 'em and eatin' bacon sandwiches and drinkin' tea. I was like something that's been locked up for a long time had been opened up and shared out. Just like things should be. I had to be at my other work in the Royal by eleven o' clock on Christmas morning. I was worried I'd be late gettin' up and that I'd feel like death warmed up, or that I might not even get up at all. But that didn't 'appen. When I got up the next morning I felt absolutely fine and I went to work as happy as a lark. We'll have to do this more often!

Gareth has always wanted to be a soldier since he was ten years old, and he must have been really keen to have left Ysgol Ardudwy at sixteen and go off to Catterick.

There's somethin' big brewin' out in the Middle East. Everyone's talking about the fifteenth of January. Gareth was saying that months ago as if the whole war had already been arranged. And there was also talk about blowin' up some of the bridges there – not the towns or the people, but destroyin' the roads and the bridges over the rivers. He said that they'd got this special equipment like you see in the fair in Barmouth designed to blow up the bridges, and we'd all be able to see it live on telly at home. Live War on CNN.

Douglas was getting on my nerves at the Carousel this morning, remindin' me how I should know more about the number 15 than anyone else in Barmouth, as I'd got a son who'd been sent out there. There was no need for that, but he was lovin' every minute, and then he goes and quotes some Welsh poem about the men who went to Catraeth which was the old Welsh name for Catterick or somethin' like that –I didn't know what the hell he was on about.

I hope my son won't have to go out there – but knowin' my luck Gareth'll get a faulty mask. I was askin' him:

"Are they givin' more lessons to you about how to deal with these chemical gases and things?"

"No more than usual," he says.

I says: "Be careful."

Why has there gotta be wars? Why does everything have to be shattered? There's always some fool who wants to do it. If something happened to my son I'd go out and hang Saddam Hussein myself. That blagard was in the telly last night, and there was talk of more and more coming over from America. They only have to show their noses and there's a war and I got a hell of shock seeing that Kate Adie out there already and dressed up like Gareth. I really hope they can get together and talk round the table before the fifteenth of January. But why are they sending so many doctors out there? They're finding it difficult to to get anyone who'll go and they're calling up all sorts out of the woodwork. Just in case.

Gareth's off to Norway, but I hope to God he isn't sent to the Gulf. It's awful for them, but what about us who are stuck back 'ere? The weather will be getting better before long and it'll all be really peaceful, maybe a bit of snow on Cadair Idris – and they'll be out there. If you see a shivering white ghostly-looking person on her way down the road at that time, it'll be me!

Bob

I'm off with the lads in the choir to sing in the Albert Hall before long. There are three buses goin' from round here this time. The biggest number yet. I thought once would be enough for me, but no – the second time was just as good and this will be my third. There's nothing like the Amen at the end of Tydi a Roddaist with the acoustics in that place. And this time we're doing a new piece – 'Y Tangnefeddwyr, the Peacemakers'.

I've been singin' for years. I used to sing for the visitors and we'd make a collection at half time for good causes. Parti Min-y-Lli we called ourselves – the seashore party – and we'd collect money for the local children's home. They managed to buy a mini bus with what we collected one year and it's still goin' strong. It's a great feeling to see 'Presented by Parti Min-y-Lli' on the back. You feel you've done something with your life. Our group was never paid any money, but in our hearts it was like winnin' the lottery.

I've got much more time to sing now too, because I've finished workin' for the Council. Retired. All I've got to do now is to watch pretty girls in the café. That's right isn't it, Marian? Marian here, well her dad used to sing with the Imperial Singers and they went to America. They published a book about them. You didn't know that, Marian? Sold well too. It'd be nice for you to have a copy to remind you of those days, wouldn't it?

The last day at work was strange. It was supposed to be comparatively light, but, hell's bells, if they didn't ask me to go and help with tarring the road near Tanygrisiau in the morning. Some old wag suggested I should have just taken a sicky – just pulling my leg like. We had a hell of a lot of laffs over the years, I'm tellin' you.

I remember some woman comin' up to me on the Cei when I was there with a skip, with a huge bag of toffee papers and asks in a really posh voice: "Can I put these in your skip?" So, I started pullin' her leg:

"You should be ashamed of yourself, madam. What do you think this is – a public dustbin?" and she rushes off in fright, with me runnin' after her. "I was only pullin' your leg, missus." I remember the big boss himself comin' down while I was tarrin' the road at Llanaber. It was a rather better day than today – I'm goin' back a good few years now when we had proper summers. Up comes this big car being driven by a man wearing enormous sun glasses:

"You didn't know me in these, did you?" he says.

So I say, "No, it's a pity you didn't put sun glasses on the car too,"

One of the last jobs I got was up in Cwm Nantcol. Just before you get to Pont y Cwm and the chapel, there's a little road leading off into the middle of the wood and if you go up that you come to the river and we had the work of carryin' a load of heavy wood from the lorry across the sheep-walk and into the forest. *Ew*, the wood weighed a ton, I can tell you. And at that time, you see, there was a war on. That's it, Marian. The Gulf. But it starts with a K... – that's it, Marian, thank you... Kuwait. And there we were buildin' this bridge in the middle of all this peace and quiet. We worked hard on that bridge, and the war goin' on and everything.

I'd like to have carved something in Welsh and English on the wood like Pont y Gwlff – just in remembrance of the lads from this area who went out there. Like Gareth from our street – he was out there and his picture was all over the front of the *Cambrian News* when he came back. He lost his mam quite suddenly then after getting back in one piece. Innocent people like her and all the anxiety she went through for nothing. Of course I couldn't have carved anything on the bridge, without it goin' through the council an' everything, but that's what I'd like to do – put Pont y Gwlff on the bridge, in memoriam. That's what I call the bridge anyway, every time I go to Cwm Nantcol. We've got to learn to build bridges in this old world, haven't we? Or we're done for. It's all about buildin' bridges, Marian. You've heard it all before, have you Marian?

Flowers

'Why do we have to bother with all these flowers at funerals?' Bryn's youthful and rather imprudent question was an emotive one for his mother sitting in the front seat. She had ordered the flowers the previous day, to ensure that they would be ready by eight 'o clock the following morning in time for the long journey down through mid Wales to one of the valleys in the south.

Bryn buttoned his lip as he watched his father carrying out the colourful wreaths in their cellophane wrappings and packing them carefully in the boot of the car. Each wreath represented the various branches of the family in the north. He could not help thinking of I.D. Hooson's poem to the uprooted daffodil – 'you'll dance no more nor hear the musician's magic pipes'. They were so perfect and beautiful – what was the point of wasting them on a day full of black shadows? Wasn't the whole reason for the journey to the south to give thanks for and to remember Aunty Gwenda's life? Bryn's expression totally betrayed his feelings.

'Flowers are important to Gwenda,' said his mother with a quiet conviction, and Bryn remained silent, trying to make sense of his mother's words.

She and Aunty Gwenda were so close, and despite the geographical distance which separated them, there was always a great sense of expectation in the weeks prior to Aunty Gwenda's visits. Aunty Gwenda had the ability to give life a shine as it were, with her natural wit and she had brought with her a great deal of light and pleasure to the big house opposite the municipal park in Aberdare.

For over twenty years her cousin had come down faithfully from the north on her annual holidays, visits which Aunty Gwenda always looked forward to. She in her turn would amble northwards in her little car, and on every occasion there would be somebody to meet her at Newtown and accompany her in convoy safely to her destination. She'd been driving since the nineteen thirties, when the roads were a lot quieter (although she never actually passed any test), and, it must be said – without wishing to be unkind, she was an appalling driver.

Her home was a huge, gentile residence in Park Lane, with a quiet couple renting part of the rear of the house. It was full of antique furniture and ancestral relics, all kept in an orderly enough manner in the rooms at the front of the house – Aunty Gwenda's rooms. Everything from childhood photographs to a bridge table, one of her favourite pastimes, and thick pile carpets.

Before being overcome and penned in by illness, hers was a cheerful if somewhat restricted existence. Her father had been a popular pharmacist in Aberdare and one of the pillars of chapel society in the area. After he died she took over the business and, by all accounts, made a very creditable job of it. She was a lifelong member of the Aberdare golf club and was inaugurated as one of their privileged officers. She was very familiar with the hotels of southern England – Bournemouth, Brighton and Bath and spent many weeks throughout her life ensconced in their lavish surroundings. However, the gallivanting and bridge parties eventually came to an end.

In her latter years a cleaner cum-carer would come in almost every day to look after her. Although she had not attended chapel for several years, she'd still send a handsome cheque every year in support of the cause right to the very end of her life. She gave help to several individuals in her own unassuming and kindly manner; privileged in material terms, she was always exceptionally kind-hearted in both word and deed.

The last time Bryn's mother stayed in Aberdare the old passion and cheerful disposition which had made her love to watch Wimbledon and golf on TV with a cigarette and cup of tea, was starting to wane. The fun and confidence with which she faced life had disappeared.

Perhaps it was the family who shared the rear of the house – and who had been a support to her on many occasion – moving to Swansea that was the last straw. She was unable to get suitable new tenants, and maybe the loneliness of the big house began to get her down. She also had to undergo major surgery at the big hospital in Merthyr and although she did manage to get to the north for a short holiday, her radiance had receded and she was losing weight from week to week. The cold frost of cancer was gradually atrophying her flesh.

When Bryn's mother took her home that time, Gwenda had insisted on going for a walk in the municipal park over the way from the house. The park was home to the *gorsedd* stones from the Aberdare Eisteddfod of 1956, but this wasn't what drew her there. She was determined to have one last look at the flowers in the park before Bryn's mother set off for the north again.

Bryn could imagine it now. The two cousins wandering slowly, arm in arm along the well-attended paths. He could see his aunt, as fragile as dried winter leaf, stepping out carefully, pointing out the different species and naming them, marvelling at their size, their colour and their beauty, fascinated by the tiniest blooms and their rainbow colours; now raising a limp arm to point to a nearby flowering shrub; offering kind words to the tireless gardeners, before returning to the house, still arm in arm, leaning heavily on his mother's shoulder.

As they drove along the Welsh border, Bryn brooded on his mother's response to his lack of enthusiasm for the funeral flowers. He remembered his mother making reference to the pleasure and wonder which his aunt would get from the miracle of the park. He felt it would be wiser for him to go along with it all and keep his mouth shut.

The car glided slowly up Park Lane, looking for the assigned parking place. The hearse was already there, its rear doors open, quietly awaiting the coffin when the service in the house was over. The flowers and the food were unloaded in a dignified manner and then the family made their way to the house. As he ascended the steps Bryn turned to view the flowers in the park through the iron railing, as they danced and smiled in the gentle tug of the breeze. He looked at them for a moment as he stood on the threshold of his aunt's house. It felt almost as if the flowers were trying to tell him something.

Bryn's mother and father entered the big room with Gwenda's sister between them, and sat on the three empty chairs in front of the silent coffin. Shortly afterwards some latecomers to the family service arrived and Bryn stood up as he saw the look on his mother's face which said 'You're the youngest here, get on your feet'. From his new vantage point he could see out of the window to the park through the white veil of the nets at half-mast, and once again his attention became fixed on the mesmerising floral dance, relieving some of the tension of having to stand for so long. They seemed to be talking, communicating, and dancing their final farewell.

Then they set off in a slow, respectful black line up to the crematorium which stood on the high ground between Aberdare and Merthyr, a large establishment with two chapels. Death can reap a heavy toll in the industrial valleys of the south. The standard service was held and a fitting tribute paid to Gwenda, the large congregation testimony to the special place she held in the hearts of all parts of Aberdare society, affluent and poor alike. As the handkerchiefs wiped the damp powder on many a cheek, the numerous wreaths of flowers shone out their presence in this final farewell, and Bryn felt that his mother had got it right.

As they drove homewards across Hirwaun, the sunset dawdling over the sheepwalks, Bryn understood his aunt's last wish that the flowers should all go to the patients in the Prince Charles hospital in Merthyr. A final opportunity for their beauty to be appreciated and a fond remembrance to her people.

Nobody said much on the way home. It had been a long and tiring day. But at some point on the journey, Bryn said in a quiet voice: 'There were a lot of flowers, Mam.'

'There were,' responded his mother. 'Your aunt loved it.'

Driftwood

It was customary for Jeanne to go to the ocean for two or three days every year. A comparatively short stay – not long enough to warrant putting her clothes in the drawers even.

"You'll have to have a look at the driftwood on the beach – a whole tree, roots an' all," Claudia told her.

Claudia was a fifty year old school teacher from San Francisco who happened to be staying in the adjoining cabin. Claudia was one of those people who would come back to the beach of her childhood; she was still recognised in this rural community. Things didn't change here. It was a place of pilgrimage, despite the fact that the occasional swell-looking buggy would go swirling past and skidding in the muscovado coloured sand, grinding up the star shells.

The driftwood was the first thing Jeanne noticed on the beach.

From the short sward of the dunes, you could see this amazing piece of flotsam dominating the beach. It was the base of an enormous tree trunk with a few roots visible, which had been carried there by the Pacific Ocean and deposited by the rushing tide flowing from Alaska.

They had spotted it initially in the evening as the sun set behind the clouds with car headlights the only real source of light remaining. Something had been left on the beach, and something else would be left there before the weekend was over. Here at the edge of the ocean, far from the hectic rush of Seattle.

On the horizon a few individual trees still remained standing, the rest of the forest that had once surrounded them ripped away.

The driftwood on the beach by the cabins at Ocean Spray Bay was indeed a remarkable specimen. Sometimes a bird would be seen perched on one of its branches, preening itself; or, on occasion, someone would be seen hiding in its shadow. There were parts of it where the bark had bee eaten away or which were black like the skin of a snake, or else bleached clean like bones. Other areas of the bark bore witness to the awful scars of a lifetime's experience. Some bits were gnarled and ugly, others beautifully smooth. Generally, the beach in the immediate vicinity of the driftwood did not attract so many people – an occasional kite-flying grandfather and grandson perhaps; or a child challenging the surf with a lobster net or surfboard, of somewhat smaller dimensions than the mighty American dream versions in California.

There was only a handful of little coastal lights to draw their attention from the here and now of their experiences over this weekend, and only the ocean to intrude on events.

In the dunes there was a house with a strange chimney which looked as if somebody was standing on the roof and leaning over. It was set back a little way off the beach in a piece of land which displayed a For Sale sign. The unstoppable modern contagion of building fever posing an obvious threat to the natural perfection of the site.

The land between the cabin and the sea, like Jeanne's young son was as yet unqualified to allow the accumulation of driftwood. Jim's experiences were yet to be lived and his horizon lay right in front of him. They rushed, like his dog's harmless forays after the birds on the foreshore. The beach itself made people open up, but the land nearby was difficult to cultivate, and would be difficult to sell. Perhaps, by some quirk of fate, it would be destined to remain for sale forever.

People would come to gather firewood there in preparation for the Pacific winter storms. Families collecting sticks with toddlers roaming on the straight road which ran down to the shore. For Jeanne it was an ideal location for a few days of contemplation. A magnificent neutral territory. The road was narrow and led straight to the beach where the sign read: 'Country Road Ends'.

Jeanne had been concerned that the weekend would slow down her packed schedule, because slowing down and stopping meant facing up to things. It was important for her to speak to her son.

Jeanne had divorced her husband and brought up her son alone, and she was about to embark on a new stage in her present job, after having felt totally undervalued in the work of constantly having to feed information into a computer. For years she had carried on with the business that had previously been run by her mother, the sale of car aircon filters to firms all along the Pacific coast. This job had concealed her real talent for poetry and psychology.

For a while after she split up with her husband and her mother died following a long illness, she had faced a difficult time of unemployment. Then she got an utterly humdrum job updating benefit forms for the elderly. But her skills with people became apparent and she was given an opportunity to exploit it when she was allowed to be involved with interviewing the elderly, something which would stretch her and relied on her amazing communications skills.

For years, because of her mother's connection with

Wales, she had been a member of the Puget Sound Welsh Choir where she found an outlet for her passion for poetry and the land of her ancestors. After a while, she sensed a certain envy in the choir, and their narrow-minded remarks concerning her relationship with another member cost her dearly.

She left the choir, as did many others, and took up a more marginal position in Welsh life on that far-flung peninsular. Although it was she who had helped to revive the Welsh community as part of Seattle's culture, there were others who had joined at a later stage with their London Welsh accents and who tried to get rid of anyone who might offer any sort of competition. By now she was also divorced from this exiled community which had originally helped her to get in touch with her roots.

"Those awful Bellevue snobs."

This weekend of self-recognition and conversing with herself in a rickety cabin by the ocean was a direct result of all this bitchiness!

She woke on the Saturday morning to the sound of coffee being ground, cartoons on the television and the dog being made a fuss of – all loud and clear through the thin walls of the cabin.

She spent her time slopping around in old clothes, walking along the beach in a mixture of drizzle or hazy sunshine.

"There's a bay full of driftwood near the native American settlement."

Claudia seemingly wanted them to see every stick of driftwood along the Washington State seaboard.

The track to the settlement turned off at the children's grave.

The Native American kids had died from some inexplicable cause. The investigation was now focussed on crop spraying.

Native Americans seemed to be burdened with such a heavy load.

To Jeanne it seemed that there were those who had to deal with some heavy and challenging problems in their lives which eventually had to be given up as driftwood, while others seemed to make such a big deal of the tiniest issue.

On the Saturday the beach revealed traces of the coastal erosion following the winter storms which had ripped out so many trees by their roots. It resembled the accumulated problems of everyone everywhere – old roots, old relics, the general messiness of people's lives.

Claudia had left by the back door and become a teacher, which involved a lot of bending over to tend to the needs of her five year old charges. Under the shadow of the Golden Gate, there was no ever-vigilant community to watch over her. Whenever she came back to her birthplace by the ocean, however, she felt at home, and that people knew her, and there was once again a sense of belonging. After spending some time here she would be ready to do a little more bending again – for the sake of the children rather than the system, of course.

"You sure sound like a great teacher to me," remarked Jeanne.

"I'm still speechless at some of these faculty meetings, and on our in-service days. They're so long and such a waste of time," was Claudia's seemingly modest reply.

With that the sound of the dog brought their thoughts back to the world of driftwood in the sunset. The dog was in the company of Jeanne's eleven year old son, Jim. He had bought fireworks at the Native American shop earlier on in the day and had brought some of them to the beach to provide a display. In the spontaneous fun of the moment, Claudia declared this to be the highlight of the evening, after her solo meal to celebrate her return at the

Dunes restaurant. She stood motionless, enjoying the cacophony of the fireworks while Jeanne covered her ears and jumped at each report.

Claudia must have been used to storms and yet still stood there speculating their aftermath.

She had witnessed another side to San Francisco which was different from the fair weather and gentle breezes which characterised its climate.

Jim was great company, a veritable firework himself, bubbling over with the energy and enthusiasm of his eleven years. Sometimes acting like an adult, sometimes like a child, the whole point of the weekend for him was to take the dog for walks, and to go to the native reservation to buy more and more fireworks. Also, in the evenings he would watch the movie series *Friday 13th* one after another on the cable channel which he could get here on the coast, Jeanne joined Jim to watch the end of the movie, and found the music beautifully relaxing. But when Jason emerged from the water in true nightmarish style, her screams could be heard echoing in the night air outside the cabin.

Every day by the ocean was like Independence Day. Jim chose to set off the fireworks next to the driftwood, their acrid smell blending with the ozone. The initials PT and FL had been carved into the bark of the trunk, like Rhys and Meinir in Nant Gwrtheyrn long ago. The fireworks were cheap things from China – an economic crutch for the Indians. They didn't last very long and flickered uncertainly in the air, some shooting off into the distance, others spluttering just a few yards before exploding in a shower of sparks. Jim also liked setting them off along the road from the cabin to the beach, marvelling at how far some of them travelled – horizontally, at times! He shot them all off into the night sky. When he got bored with that, he began placing them with their noses buried in the ground, creating small explosions, but which made little real impression on the general structure of the sand.

"Inside I'm still like Jim," Jeanne explained to Claudia.

The beach was also quite familiar to Jeanne. Her mother having family connections with the area. She remembered how the family used to be able to get wonderful oyster sandwiches on their way to the ocean in the famous *salon* at Olympia.

Back in Seattle, Jeanne had a partner who was too nice a guy according to his superiors to sell advertising, and his job was now on the line. He was not aggressive enough.

Jeanne was already preparing herself for facing up to going back after the weekend, and probably the need to cheer him up. The new bosses were making things difficult for him – asking him to increase his sales, reducing his basic salary, but increasing the bonus to be earned from making more sales.

Anton understood Jeanne, and Jeanne was someone who needed to hear people saying that to her on a fairly regular basis. Anton was a good man, courteous to a fault, but a certain hard-nosed cynicism had taken up residence and he was strongly opposed to all types of organised religion. Such an attitude aggravated by a constant negative sense of humour could undermine, but not change, Jeanne's inherently gracious nature.

Discussing a possible break-up, with Claudia, was a valuable exercise. In divorcing her husband, Rod, Jeanne had split up with her childhood sweetheart, who had ultimately become Jim's dad. Having divorced him, they had become better friends after the hurt had subsided. With Jim to bring up, there was no time for bitterness or negative energy. She had had a lot on her plate – caring for her mother – who was dying – but somehow or other she had emerged the other side of her ordeal.

Sure, it hurt when her friends got invitations to her ex-husband's second marriage and some of them were even vicious enough to show her the invitations. But she managed to maintain her self-respect, manifesting the dignity imbued in her Native American bloodline on her father's side.

Anton lived on a boat on Lake Washington and he too had been through a divorce but had no children. There was no pressure on him to be a family man, which brought back old ghosts and the old tapes which had played in his head for so long. Jeanne had to wait for a long time before she knew exactly the right way to play this. She was not completely convinced although he occupied a fairly prominent place in her life in the city as it was. Anyway, she could pretend that she was pretty content. She wanted him to share with her and yet, sometimes, he could be as cold as ice and then suddenly warm again.

The key incident which had really shaken her was when he failed to congratulate her on her recent promotion. Such an important day for her – and he hadn't even called her.

"I want to be the most important thing in his life, but I don't want to know if that's possible. It's that old see-saw again – stopping me from giving my all. There's a lot of questions that haven't been answered."

She had to decide that weekend whether it was all worth the effort. And whether she'd have to tell Jim.

The TV was intruding again for the second night running, as the cable network was showing a full weekend of *Friday 13th* movies.

"What's this *Friday 13th,* part 27, Jim? I don't know why they haven't filled in Crystal Lake with gravel after the first one, and buried Jason in it at the same time."

No one but Jim could face the ordeal and for a while

the screams disturbed her sleep, until eventually even Jim got fed up and stopped watching.

"How was the movie?"

"They ate him for a snack and spat him out."

Jeanne felt very close to her son here by the ocean, close to his sense of humour and fun. The only one who came close to that idea of fun, she had to admit, was Anton. As a child she used to come to this area and stay in cabins like this a little further down the coast and visit her aunt and uncle.

In fact, just down the coast was Claudia's Driftwood Bay, full of memories and unfulfilled longing. Driftwood Bay. A beach full of huge pieces of driftwood. These were not victims of erosion but instead had been carried by the tide and hurled onto the beach in the frenzy of the winter storms. Behind the bay, there were paths which ran through thickets of wild blackberries and other edible fruits, delicious fillings for pies such as those served to Claudia at the *Dunes* restaurant.

Driftwood experiences – big, small, selfish or irrelevant. The ocean offered such consolation, prepared to take on board their shame or guilt and to dilute it and soothe it; to take away the pain on a tide of love. The driftwood – big and small alike – would eventually be gathered up by the tide. But the single piece of driftwood near the wooden cabin was quite enough for Jeanne after seeing all the flotsam in the renowned eponymous bay down the coast.

Jeanne thought of Anton spending his Sunday evening wandering the university quarter of Bellevue, looking for bargains in the second-hand bookstores – anything to forget about Monday morning.

He'd probably revive his flagging spirits by recalling the guitar chords for *House of the Rising Sun* and other songs from the sixties. He'd be leading the singing of these songs in his imagination, a beat at a time as he drove back to his houseboat...

Unlike Anton dreading the prospects of Monday morning and the hard-sell routine which faced him, Jeanne, in her new post, would not now have to get up at five 'o clock to catch a bus at six. For the first time when she returned from this break, she would be able to catch the quarter past seven bus to reach her work by eight and be dealing with real live people and not just with dumb machines and e-mail.

"I can look at the driftwood – the colours in the bark and the blackness around it – and think about that image. That image was around generations ago and people would notice the same thing, and the link would be made – the sense of belonging. Nowadays, you grab a plastic cup of latte at seven in the morning and everyone's drinking one as they go up the escalator to the office – not engaging with anyone or anything."

The main conversation of the weekend took place in the translucent darkness, in the early hours of Monday morning.

"Jim, I can really goof around in front of you, and yet I can also reveal things about myself which it would be difficult to do with anyone else. I respect you so much, and I want this to sound right. I want you to know, if I get married to Anton, that doesn't make any difference to us. I just wanted you to know that."

Jim accepted his fate quite quietly.

Jim had left the remains of the fireworks together with a couple of empty Diet Coke tins on the beach near the driftwood, and on the last morning he promised to collect up his trash in a bag, all of it – the shattered remains of old dreams and long memories of frail bits of timber, the extinguished hopes of burnt-out sparklers – he promised to gather them up and clean up the place leaving the driftwood as they had found it. But by the time Monday morning arrived, he had forgotten his environmental commitments. Jim was still too young to leave anything lasting in the shadow of the driftwood where generations had endeavoured to carve their messages.

There was still time for Jim to enjoy youth's colourful firework display and Claudia and Jeanne required a little intuitive confidence and enthusiasm to find new ways and fresh pastures. Both women were holding back, looking for the way forward.

Jim had experimented with putting lighter fuel into a Diet Coke tin and then igniting the contents, unaware of the danger. The fireworks had shot off in all directions. Jim's eyes lit up with each whizzing rocket.

Everyone loved Jim.

By a total coincidence his best friend and his brothers were going to camp in the Cascade Range. He was happy enough to eat his Fruit on a stick and to carve his name on the steps of the cabin. He would be quite content on the way home too, sticking his head out of the window and declaring "It's happening" to any other cars around, despite his mother's incessant pleas for him not to do this.

Jim despite his outward banter and enthusiasm was too young to leave any driftwood behind. Someone else would come along and clear it all up, he mused as he lay in bed that morning.

Jeanne set off alone on one final hike down to the driftwood, picking up the occasional bits of unsightly trash along the way and placing them in the plastic bag which had contained the fireworks from the shop. She realised that much of it was paper which would breakdown naturally anyway, and yet there would be some of it which would take years to degrade and would be an obstacle to a free-running child full of ideals. The tide always seemed to be coming in and the driftwood offered possibilities.

The previous night's drizzle had reduced the remains of the fireworks into a pulpy mush and the sand had already buried much of the detritus. But some of the larger items still caught up on the trunk. An old box of bangers, spent fat-bellied fireworks which were previously so full of hope; plastic ribbons – a stream of futile aspirations. She gathered them all up into the plastic bag to dispose of them forever. The driftwood was ready to be abandoned.

They were still those who believed in the Legend of the Star Shells here – they didn't want the centre to be ripped out by gulls. Legends still existed even if people shied away from them.

The sun rose through the branches of the shattered tree, shining on the dew and raindrops of an overnight shower. Bird calls pricked the dunes. The communion had been renewed. Echoes of her conversation with Jim during the night back in the cabin dispersed her fears. The dawn had broken. All that remained was the triumphant roar of the ocean. The driftwood had been given up and abandoned.

The Café

A dramatic presentation for 6 characters adapted from the novel Y CAFFI.

CHARACTERS.

Dai Owen – an old gentleman from Rhos
Pauline – Former guide at Yale Hall.
Crosswords – A strait-laced old man who is fond of doing crosswords whilst sitting on public benches.
Jessica – A middle aged artistic woman.
Ryan – Former steelworker, who opens a gymnasium called "Muscles".
Jan – a cleaner at the local Video and Record Library

THE CHARACTERS ENTER, TAKING THEIR PLACE AT INDIVIDUAL TABLES IN THE CAFÉ. EACH MONOLOGUE CAN BE LINKED BY MUSIC, OR THE WAITRESS COMING AND GOING TO AND FROM THE TABLES.

DAI OWEN 1.
DAI IS AN OLD MAN AND HAS A WHITE STICK. HE CAN PRESENT HIS MONOLOGUE AS IF HE WERE PREACHING IN ONE OF THE NUMEROUS OLD CHAPELS OF RHOS. HE BELIEVES HE IS BACK IN THE RHOS OF YESTERYEAR – SOCIALIST AND CHAPEL-GOING. AN ECHO EFFECT COULD BE USED WHEN HE SPEAKS

The worst word ever created is the word Me. All for one and all for me. Me, me, me. And until we learn to say We, this world will never come back to its senses. We measure everything on the Me scale – even our good deeds. Go and pick someone up, give them a lift to chapel so that people can say that we're always doin' good deeds and helpin' others.
-- He's a good man. We only do things so that people will create miniature gods of us.

DAI LEANS FORWARD.

The Family is finished now. When I was small all the family would be there on a Sunday night in chapel – not sending the children late to Sunday School and going to shop in Lo-Cost. Years ago everyone in Rhos would go to the Hymn Singing Festival in Calfaria in January. They won't cross the road now. They've forgotten about the woman with the hatling today. At the time of the Strike nobody starved in Rhos – everyone shared and cared for one another, but now in Rhos and every other Rhos, there's locks on all the doors. And then there's the Stiwt – the colliers donated a penny a week to build it, and their wages didn't stretch very far. Long ago the people next door used to ask you if you wanted anything when you weren't well.

How many people in Town today long for someone to call round, so that they are not all by themselves all day?

JAN – 1.

JAN IS CLEANING THE RECORD, CD AND VIDEO SECTION OF THE LOCAL COMMUNITY VIDEO LIBRARY. SHE IS IN HER LATE FORTIES, A LITTLE OVERWEIGHT AND HER HAIR IS DYED A VIVID RED.

I tell 'em in the Community Video – don't apologise for the rubbish and the dust. It mounts up in the middle of old records and films, and there's so many of 'em ! Old tapes lyin' around. I got old tapes turnin' in my 'ead by now, let alone anywhere else. But if there weren't no dirt, there'd be no work for me. But there's muck **an'** muck isn't there ?

JAN IS DUSTING SOME CD'S WITH A BRIGHTLY COLOURFUL CLOTH OR FEATHER DUSTER. SHE PAUSES TO THINK.

I'm startin' to stick up for myself now – now that I'm forty four and my knee's startin' to ache. I hop along this place like Long John Silver! Sometimes I don't know which is best – security or independence. At the moment I like independence that teeny bit more. When I'm at home havin' a nice bath or all cosy and warm in my bed, I think, ooh, I like this. At other times I think that there's somethin' missin', somethin' I'm used to.

I came to this Community Video as a favour to the Boss, 'cos I've known him for years – since I was a little girl. I could tell you a few stories about him. We were both brought up poor in large families, and he's done well – you've got to 'and it to him. When I first came here I thought his Secretary was a real stuck up bitch, but then she was lookin' for someone to clean for her 'cos she'd be workin' late in the office every night an' 'er 'usband wantin' a clean white shirt pressed every day – she jus' couldn't cope with it all. That's when I saw the other side of 'er – when she said she wanted someone to clean, someone she could trust.

Well I couldn't do it on top of everythin' else, but I asked my eldest daughter. But what had pleased me more than anything was that she'd trusted me. She'd asked **me**. It's difficult, but I'm startin' to get to know myself, and it's a good experience.

PAULINE 1

PAULINE DRESSES WELL AND IS IN HER LATE FIFTIES. AS SHE DOESN'T SEE MANY PEOPLE SHE TENDS TO TALK INCESSANTLY. FORMERLY, SHE WORKED IN YALE HALL, A LOCAL HOUSE OF HISTORICAL INTEREST, UNTIL THERE WAS SOME SORT OF DISAGREEMENT. SHE IS STUDYING THE YALE HALL GUIDE BOOK FOR THE NEW SEASON

They've spoilt Yale Hall. I went to the official opening for the new Season. They want money, money, money. They want it all ways. I like what the Trust does to old buildings, but they should realise what they are doing to *people*. Realise who's really loyal to them at the end of the day. You've got young slips of girls coming there and getting fast-track promotion. I was in the Ticket Office one day and the Big Boss himself comes in looking very despondent, and I said flippantly

– How are these young ones getting on as Guides?

– The young ones are alright; the old ones are the problem.

I couldn't believe my ears. I've heard these schoolgirls talking to people going around the Hall

– Don't go that way

– Not over there

when

– Excuse me, but do you mind not going over there sounds so much better. And most of them aren't local people who know the Hall, but people from away who want to be seen. So I've decided not to volunteer this year, while the current incumbents are at the helm.

CROSSWORDS – 1.

CROSSWORDS IS A STRAIT-LACED OLD MAN WHO SPENDS HIS DAYS ON PUBLIC BENCHES IN TOWN, CHATTING WHEN HE CHOOSES, BUT MORE IMPORTANT THAN ANYTHING TO HIM, COMPLETING HIS NEWSPAPER CROSSWORDS. HE PARTICULARLY ENJOYS THE BENCH NEAR THE CAFE. THE BENCH COULD POSSIBLY BE ON A LOWER LEVEL.

These town benches are funny places. In the winter, nobody's interested in them, but come summer every Tom, Dick and Harry comes out of the woodwork, and rushes to sit on them. Sweethearts eating each other alive in broad daylight. Common lot. But I must admit I'm glad to see the sun after this last long winter.

I was frightened in the middle of all that snow. It took me back to 1947 and the farm in Llanwddyn, and Dad having to cut his way through the snow to take the body of a four year old girl to be buried. Every day I look in the Daily Post – I read the deaths column in case my name has slipped in there somehow.

No, I'm gettin' too old. That Christmas service with the young people in chapel nearly finished me off. That young soloist was singing as if she was in a Club in Pontins Prestatyn. No, I'm angry with them in Capel y Graig. There's no decency and decorum left, and certainly there's no room for an electric guitar in worship. But there we are, I've always been a formal and old fashioned type, even when I was a spring chicken with the Baptists in Caersws. I'm a bit like Mrs Bouquet, in a world which is sadly full of Onslows. Full of cowboys. But you must have formality, after all what else have we got to offer? The Organ brings decorum to the House of God.

DAI OWEN – 2

The mind is the best diary – and although there's only a little time left for me, there's very much more to look back on – and that's where my hope lies. While my memory remains intact, it means I'm still alive. I had the privilege of living in Rhos in the golden era.

And that's all gone. It's my fault and others like me who didn't go back. That's what it is. Why do I live in Town? It'd be better if I was in Rhos, but it saddens me to see the place today. Drugs being sold on street corners *uffen*. Years ago Rhos people had three things – Chapel, Stiwt and The Hafod. Actually calling the place Rhos today is an insult to the past. Where have all the characters gone? Years ago you could single them out – **Dacw gymeriad.** But nobody's got substance today. And before you start, it's **me** that's saying this about Rhos *enai*, not some newcomer. Me. I've got a right to. I joke with the people in Town and tell them they need a passport on Gutter Hill, and even then it's subject to our approval.

In the twenties Calfaria Chapel had a debt of eight hundred and twenty one pounds, and they had an Appeal to keep the doors open. People were selling their pigs, and colliers were giving their money. People preferred to go without rather than see the chapel suffering. The debt was cleared by Sunday afternoon, and with the money that was left they made some commemorative mugs to mark the sacrifice, and to celebrate clearin' the debt. Nobody would do that today. On a Sunday you're lucky if you get six in a cold vestry keepin' the place goin', with the odd concert to collect money. The place is full for a concert. And let me say this, wherever Caradog Roberts might be on a Saturday, he was there at the organ on a Sunday. That was a sense of duty.

The Ministers were the voice of the workers and the union at that time. They'd be marching with the miners during the Strike, they'd work right in the middle of the ills of society. (PAUSE) All that lies in the graveyard now. We inherited all this from that society, but where did it go once we became educated? – **How are you?** is what you get now, if you're lucky, not – **Lle ti di bod yn cuddio, uffern ?**

JESSICA – 1

JESSICA CAN BE SEEN STRUGGLING WITH SOME BAGS AT THE TABLE, OR IN FLASHBACK TO HER SINGLE-BEDROOM FLAT WHERE SHE STRUGGLES WITH HER HOOVER. SHE DROPS EVERYTHING AND SITS DOWN FOR HER HERBAL TEA.

Dirk Bogarde jumped the queue in my writing list. He beat Aunt Madge, and Brenda, the poet from Vancouver. I was there eating my morning muesli when he came on

Radio Four reading his autobiography "A Short Walk from Harrods". Well, it was brilliant – it was so riveting that I put down my slice of brown wholemeal toast and Flora. I was glued to my seat, and I even stopped chewing because it was detracting from the story.

He was describing these rather superficial people in this posh dinner party – one woman who'd just had a nose job, another one playing with the mousse on her plate. Obviously he was accepted there, but he could see through the pretence of it all.

– You don't live in Knightsbridge? one of the women asked him, and then he describes the old bitch saying

– Well, at least you live within a stone's throw of Harrods.

I was jumping about on my rickety old chair by this time. His words were so gripping that I forgot any need to shop or to clean the flat – you know, all those things that Mummy worries about.

I went straight to the typewriter. I put in the paper and proceeded to write Dirk a letter praising his story. I used rather a good image, even though I say it myself – I told him that his work cut like a knife, and cut me up into little pieces of flesh on the block. Well it sounded better than that in the letter. I told him that I'd like a liaison via mail with him, because we were similar souls.

DAI OWEN – 3.

My old mate, Jim, knew what poverty was – but when we used to go out to play with one another as children we didn't notice any differences. I didn't think twice about giving him a piggy-back to school because of his bare feet. That was Rhos for you. We all had the same start in life. If I'd been a bad boy my Dad would send me to bed straight from school for a whole week – he never laid a hand on me, but he knew what had the desired effect.

And if I was later than four o clock coming for tea on a Sunday afternoon I went without, because Mam had to have a bit of a break before going to chapel at six. Dad used to recite an old verse :

"Rhanna dy bethau gorau
Rhanna â thi yn dlawd...
...Rhyw eiddo bach yw eiddo'r dyn
sy'n cadw'i nefoedd iddo'i hun."

Something like that. But it says it all about sharing. It's by one of the old masters, but I forget which one now.

DAI COULD LOOK THROUGH THE FAMILY BIBLE.

RYAN – 1

RYAN WAS A STEEL WORKER AT BRYMBO STEEL, WHERE HE WORKED AFTER LEAVING YSGOL BRYN ALYN. HIS FORMER CO-WORKER, SELWYN, IS WELSH-SPEAKING AND HAS TALKED ABOUT HIS INTEREST IN WELSH FOLK SONGS AND CHOIR SONGS TO RYAN AS THEY WORKED THE FOUNDRY.
RYAN IS IN HIS EARLY THIRTIES, GOOD-LOOKING WITH BLONDE STREAKED HAIR AND EARRINGS. HE IS FIT AND IS WEARING FASHION-ABLE TRAINING GEAR – PERHAPS WITH THE LOGO OF THE NEWLY-ESTABLISHED GYM "CYHYRAU" ON A T-SHIRT. WHEN WE FIRST MEET HIM HE IS LIFTING SOME HAND WEIGHTS. DIFFERENT APPARATUS CAN BE USED.

I had to take the bull by the 'orns, like. That's what I did. You need a bit of muscle to open a place like CYHYRAU – a gym and fitness centre. I'd 'oped to open somethin' for the local kids when the lease on Brymbo village hall came up, but my bid was refused. I don't understand things like that, especially when you've lived in the area all your life. So I went out on my own, and opened this gym on the little industrial estate they've started in the village.

I worked so 'ard getting' the place ready, and before I realised it, the apparatus was all in place, and I'd opened shop. *Duw*, I love being my own boss, no more working shifts and nights. When I worked in Brymbo, the steelworks dominated my whole life.

PAULINE – 2.

In the early days at Yale Hall, we'd go to the Refectory before our stint as stewards, and we'd have a cup of coffee and a scone. Now the scone's gone, and you'll get a coffee when and if you're lucky – usually when you're on your knees. The Refectory isn't everything it's cracked up to be. When Felicity came to stay with me at the flat I took her there, and I paid over sixteen pound for soup, a croissant with a Welsh cheese filling, and a piece of Bakewell that was like cardboard.

I remember once, I arrived at break time, and I had to borrow a pound from that spooky lady on the registration desk, because I'd forgotten my money that day. I went armed with this pound to the Refec to have a coffee, and I felt an ice cream coming on.

– Will you sit down love, it's waitress service.

– But I only want an ice cream.

– Before I go any further... have I got enough money to buy an ice cream?

The management of the Hall has become two tiered, totally at odds with the ethos of the noble family who used to live there. But there we go – the people who want to create an "us" and "them" get all the plum jobs these days. Of course the Boss spoils the place – he wants instant cash from day visitors, and yet he wants more full-time members for the Trust. He wants it all ways. Don't they make you sick? And yet, surprise surprise, he doesn't want all these visitors going through the house ruining the carpets – over 90,000 of them last season, and yet he wants 95,000 visitors next year, and a 100,000 the year after. Some tourism performance tables or other he called it. So he's devised two trips – one to the gardens and shop, and the other to the house, garden and shop. All roads lead to the shop, obviously.

And the teachers who come there – I don't know who they think they are. Sometimes, in front of a gaggle of little ones, they point to a picture and say: **This is a Gainsborough.** On the other hand some point and say: **This is a big picture.**

Thank goodness the National Curriculum has kicked in, to give everyone the same education. It was long overdue to weed poor teachers out of the education system.

JAN – 2

It was difficult 'cos **he** lived around the corner, and they'd go by in the new car, the one he bought originally for us two. That used to hit me every single day, as if my dreams were going to and fro, to and fro. Until they stopped being dreams. But I didn't let it show on the surface that it was havin' any affect on me at all.

I made a New Year's resolution that I wouldn't love again, and I went as cold as ice, but now maybe I'm startin' to thaw out a little. But it would have to be someone who loved me totally – after twenty seven years of marriage it was hard. Losin' the security. It's only now that I'm findin' my feet – two years after the split. I know it sounds an awful thing to say, but where I found my feet, he didn't find 'is. I don't want a man in my life. Stay single, that's what I tell Noel in this studio, and he always blushes. It's less hassle for you, darlin'.

CROSSWORDS – 2

Keep your own counsel, that's what I say. I don't want to see everything. No. I certainly don't want to be tied to by some narrow-minded deacons with their ideas for a chapel dinner club. Eating at twelve all together – I want to eat when I want to eat, and then a plateful of fried stuff. It was different when I lived on the farm. But I won't be ruled by any Satan in saintly guise, these whited sepulchres. The minute you let Old Nick in, he gets hold of you, you know!

Methodistiaid creulon cas
yn mynd i'r capel heb ddim gras.

That's what the old rhyme had to say about the Calvinists. Well, to hell with the lot of them – Pope is the one for me, the one and only Pope **"Hope springs eternal in the human breast".**

PAULINE – 3

PAULINE TAKES SOME PHOTOGRAPHS OUT OF A PACKAGE SHE HAS JUST PICKED UP. SHE PLACES THEM ON THE COFFEE TABLE.

I've just come back from a holiday on the Rhine in Germany, where the eating arrangements were like a Sunday school party. Every six places there was a biro mark on the table to show where the vegetables had to stretch to. And woe betide if you crossed the border, as it were! If there were a few potatoes left the waiters would grab them straight away to be used again. Felicity looked better after getting a whiff of the breeze on the Rhine.

147

That's where Richard Burton used to come to 'dry out' so they say.

I'm glad the Lorelei went better than Landudno. Felicity took a tumble in Happy Valley that left me up a gum tree all week. She was all of a quiver on the Great Orme, but she's saying already that she'd like to go to the Turkey and Tinsel in the Ambassador next Christmas. Perhaps the trams will be up and running by then, running on some of the old tracks from the past. Even now I love walking between the Bandstand and the Hydro.

PAULINE LOOKS OUT THROUGH THE WINDOW. IT IS MORNING AND PEOPLE ARE RUSHING TO THE NEARBY SCHOOL.

There she goes again. That lovely lady from those lovely new houses in the trees. I'm sure she's an asset to them at the secondary school. Someone said, she's got a real welcome for everyone when you go there. I'm sure she does too.

PAULINE WAVES.

We just wave every morning. Sometimes I mouth "How are you?" and she mouths back "Okay, thanks", or else she clutches her throat if she's got a sore throat. It's good to be able to wave at someone nice. The people in my new block of flats are fine, although it's really strange not having your own house anymore. There's a man in the bottom flat at the end who used to keep a shop down the road from Cilla Black. It's Cilla this and Cilla that with him. Well, I'm sure it's alright living near her, as long as you don't have to listen to her singing. Then the rest are all elderly people – and before you say it – are they trying to tell me something, this all-knowing council? And the lady at the top end – everyone used to make a funny gesture behind her back as if she was one sandwich short of a picnic, but when I sent her a Christmas card I got a lovely letter back from her. She likes a bit of peace and quiet, that's what it is. She's a bit like me. But having mentioned Cyril always talking about Cilla, I did get a Christmas present through the letter box in a Marks and Spencers bag – a pair of gloves from him and two kisses from Cilla, the dog. Well, at least they think something of me.

RYAN – 2

I've realised that there's a whole new world out there, beyond the steel works, and it's great. I'd been there ever since I left Bryn Alyn School, and I never saw any further than its boundaries – I couldn't even see the bright lights of the big bad town below us. I only saw those on the odd steamin' Saturday night. Clubbin'. When the Works shut down it was either a blessin' or a curse. But when I heard about the redundancy pay-off I grabbed it.

They were full of some fancy courses for a year to relocate you in employment, so that you could 'branch out', diversify, but I hadn't got the patience to go on a course and then find there was no work at the end of it, so here I am! Some are still lordin' it on these dead end courses, and here am I listenin' to Olivia Newton John singin' Let's Get Physical. I took the plunge.

JAN – 3

The other mornin' there was human shit on the floor of the men's toilets – in the pub where I clean twice a week first thing. I couldn't believe it, and there was no reason why I should be the one to clear it up. I was heavin'. I did clear it up tho'. But I decided that I wasn't here to clear shit again. I've gor enough of it in my own life already, thank you very much. The bastards wouldn't act like that at 'ome. I've got better things to do than clear up shit. That's not my job.....Hey that's a good pun. Job. Get it ?

Anyway, the landlord who's another old friend from long ago, went ballistic, and he wrote this note and stuck it on the door of the men's bogs :

Would the dirty slovenly bastard who shits all over the floor care to clean up after himself? P.S. In case you have difficulty reading this note, below is a translation into your mother tongue. Grunt, grunt, grunt, grunt, grunt!

I suspect that it was him what did it in the first place – the old bugger. But I need the money. So I'm saying nowt.

PAULINE – 4

Little things have changed at Yale House. Give someone a badge and it goes straight to his head. Anyway, I've heard that the staff disappear as soon as they come. It's like the Ten Green Bottles standing on the wall. The sort of people who volunteer to become stewards at Yale House don't deserve this kind of treatment. I was telling Felicity about it in the Conservative Club.

She's had quite a rocky year with one thing and another – especially after the fall in Happy Valley. It sounds funny doesn't it – a fall in Happy Valley? As if redemption is out of bounds. But I love Landudno, and as far as I'm concerned they can bring back those trams tomorrow. Listening to the sound of the trams when I was wrapped up all warm in my hotel bed was a special part of my childhood. Anything that reminds me of that time, I'm for it. Life was one huge tea party then.

There's no poetry like Melin Trefin and Clychau Cantre'r Gwaelod nowadays. No Cwm Pennant and no bells of Aberdyfi – I was thinking about the Bells of Aberdyfi one night – it was goin' round in my head all night. (PAUSE)

"Nid yw'r felin heno'n malu
Yn Nhrefîn ym min y môr."

I don't understand this modern stuff. You wouldn't find anything about old Wil in the gaol in Ruthin in it.

"Mae Wil yng Ngharchar Rhuthun
a'i wraig yn malio dim"

– not in those plain terms anyway. It would have to be full of long fancy words that no one understands. I remember Wordsworth's Daffodils and Macbeth – **"Out brief candle, out!"**

The things I learnt at home on the hearth are my memories now. My father always used to say "Plant seeds when you're young, so that you'll have shelter when you're old". He had a good head on him, my Dad, although I argued like the **"cyndiar"** with him when he was alive. Young people today don't plant anything. But it's the memories that keep me alive ... that's why I'm still here....the memories that were planted long ago.

Jim is on my mind today. Jim came into this life alone and departed from it alone. He loved comin' into the Café every Thursday with his memories. **"Ti'n cofio hwn? Ti'n gwbad. Oedd o'n byw yn ymyl...."** and his memory was alive on the map of the past. What will today's children have to remember?

After you'd been down the Hafod every day for twelve hours, the only thing worth thinking about was heaven. Chapels large and small – *mawr a bychan* – meant somethin' then. Now people only know where the chapels are, and that's if you're lucky. They don't attend them but they'll tell you where they are. "Near the video shop *uffen*, next door to the Take Away."

JESSICA – 2

I don't know whether the letter even reached Dirk Bogarde, I'm sure he receives hundreds. Perhaps when he read the bit about meat being cut up on the block, I'm sure he started thinking, "Golly – Who the hell have I got here?" But I heard him saying one day on Radio Four that he has written for years to some woman, even though he's never met her, and that a certain kind of love has developed between them.

Hey, what if **I** had an answer? What if Dirk bloody well wrote to me for a change? What if he said that he was popping over to discuss Literature? It would give the odd bloody crowd in this cul-de sac some food for thought – something worth talking about in Prozac Close. Oh, the bloody curtains would be twitching more than usual if Dirk Bogarde walked down the close with a copy of his latest bestseller under his arm, and if he came up my concrete stairs and knocked on the door of my flat. That would give the gossips plenty of scope. There'd be headlines in the Evening Leader. Getting a reply from Dirk would make me do the hoovering. I'd have it done in no time. Give the flat a spanking, as Mummy says. I'd face the mountain of washing up then, like that woman with soft hands in the Fairy Liquid advert.

> **Thus let me live, unseen, unknown,**
> **Thus lamented let me die,**
> **Steal from the world, and not a stone**
> **Tell where I lie.**

Alexander Pope. Remember those words and remember the Apostle Paul. **I ran the race.** ***Ymdrechais ymdrech deg.*** I've done my best, what more can we do? More than that and we'd all be knackered. I'm sounding like Onslow now.

CROSSWORDS CONSULTS HIS DAILY MAIL AND STARTS THE CROSSWORD.

It's so difficult being original – everyone likes the same things today. The creakiest gates last longest though. I have an Aunt who moans her life away, but she's still here. In fact she's still going strong in Ellesmere. She'll be here after all of us. (PAUSE)

Once, I went to see Danny La Rue's drag act. I expected him to act like a lady, not like a dirty slut using foul language. (PAUSE)

And everyone's eating fruit wanting to be ever so slim. I don't listen to the Satanists. But I do get so limp in this hot weather.

CROSSWORDS LOOKS CONTEMPLATIVE, SHOW-ING A HINT OF A MORE TENDER SIDE.

Those youngsters on that bench over there have thrown some bread to the birds – but they've thrown it too close to the road. The little birds are frightened to go too close to the road.

Apart from that nice woman who looks like Ruth Madoc from Capel y Graig, I haven't got much to say to religion – and as for Evangelicals and the Happy Clappy Hippie Brigade – don't get me on my soap box. Restraint in all things. Moderation.

Well I'm off now to buy a National Lottery ticket. Try and keep cool! *Hwyl a Heddwch!*

RYAN – 3

LIFTING SOME WEIGHTS.

Weight-lifting was only an interest for me – in work it was part of the job, and everyone who comes to the Club does it naturally. I can't stop them taking steroids at home, but here at the gym they can buy protein drinks and Liquid Liver, and things like that to strengthen their bodies.

All sorts come here – it's quite interesting to observe them, to tell you the truth – to people watch. This is the first chance I've had to do that. To observe people. You've got the Beginners, some come to lift the heavy weights, really heavy – heavier than me. A lot of women come just to work out, but the blokes come to develop the muscles. Because there's a membership fee we don't get any cowboys here who are playin' about, and I've had a range of clothing made with the official name of the club on them, and they're sellin' quite well. Everybody wants to know what "CYHYRAU" means. I needed 'cyhyrau' to open this place I can tell you. Selwyn told me that CYHYRAU was Welsh for Muscles, and I liked the sound of the word.

JAN – 4

I've still got **his** photos in the house. The other night I was knittin' – I do orders for people and *Saved by the Bell by the Bee Gees* came on the tape, and I just had to brush the tears from my eyes and say "Stick at it, girl".

I'm the weakest person who ever lived – I love too much, if there's such a thing, and yet my friends think

I've been strong now, and my girls do as well – the four of 'em. And in some way I suppose I have been strong.

JAN LOOKS THROUGH OLD RECORDS AND DUSTS OLD VIDEOS.

You see my brother died, and we were very close – he was a lovely boy full of humour and he always used to make me laugh. This coincided with the first time my husband left, and I knew I had to bury my feelings down deep inside me to be able to cope with everythin' that was goin' on. God only made one of my brother, and then he threw away the mould. (PAUSE) I'd never 'ad a proper Dad, so I loved my brother. He used to tell me stories and sing funny songs. I was five and he was twelve. His ashes were scattered all over the Kop in Old Trafford. We should have been on Surprise Surprise with Cilla really because it was a tremendous experience.

DAI OWEN – 5

In Rhos, years ago, I lived **here** and Jim lived **there** – and they were two different worlds, which saw things from different perspectives. He lived in a tŷ siambar in Pentrefelin, and at that time Pentrefelin was different to the rest of Rhos – the people there knew poverty. His Mam and Dad died, and Jim went into care. Jim died alone, but he was richer than me because he knew what poverty really was. He's seen that side of the fence. *Ochr ene'r wal.* He was given food here and there in the days when chapel vestries offered assistance. He remembered people's kindness at the time of the Strike, and remembered goin' down to Ruabon, cap in hand.
– Caled yw fy nhamaid bara...
I was fortunate – I had the support of parents – but Jim didn't go to Grammar School. There were several like him – I remember Harri Bellis – there were more

155

brains in his little finger than there were in my head –
but his Dad drank every night, and at fourteen years of
age talent like that went down Gresford. It was a tragedy
and a waste of life, because Harri Bellis was killed, and
he was a truly talented person, but then someone like me
had a chance to get on in life.

JESSICA – 3

JESSICA TAKES ANOTHER SIP OF HER TEA. THE
HERBAL TEA BAG REMAINS IN THE CUP.

The children come and see me, but it's only very
occasionally, but not nearly enough. They think I'm mad
because I'm a writer. Sometimes they bring my lovely
little grandchildren with them. I usually catch a bus to
Plas Offa on a Friday, although it hurts to go back to the
old domain of my marriage and to remember the time
when we were a whole family together. Why was I so
stupid as to let the whole thing slip through my fingers?

This story on the radio – Dirk's story- went on. He was
going around the supermarket thinking "What can I
have for tea?" and he was thinking on the same lines as
me – if I have a bowl of mushroom soup it'll mean that I
only have to wash a bowl and a spoon, and so on. Then
his food trolley goes crash into the one of this bombastic
woman with her hair in a bun, who argues with him
about her place in the checkout queue. Then the Store
Manager spots this and calls over
– Would you like to step this way, my Lord? And that
puts her in her place. We need to put some of these people
in their places.

RYAN – 4

I'm amazed where the customers come from – it's not the local lads so much 'cos they're too busy on these dead end courses to be able to come now. Five come over from Buckley, and some from Town because the prices are quite reasonable. There's a feeling of belongin' here, and it's a thing that's developin', this Keep Fit, and we're still a community up here despite closin' the steel works. They weren't able to thrash that out of us, and the Works was making a profit too.

RYAN DOES SOME PRESS-UPS OR AN EXERCISE.

I've just put up another mirror. I could see it all in my head, but I had to wait for some money to flow in so that I could buy it, and I put the toilets and the showers in myself. I had a bit of difficulty with the roof, and there was a lot of swearin' in the air above Tanyfron and Southsea that night, you bet! The air was blue. It's a long workin' day, but the hours fly from eleven till nine at night. The place gets very busy after six, when people come from work, if there's still work out there. It's heavin' here sometimes.

CROSSWORDS – 4

CROSSWORDS IS LOOKING AT A NEWLY- ERECTED MODERN SCULPTURE.

I don't think much of this new sculpture by the bench – they call these things 'Art' – well I don't. What next? I remember an exhibition in Liverpool where there was a sack of coal emptied in the middle of a room and then the sack flung willy-nilly to one side. Have you ever heard of such a thing? And another one was these sheets chucked on top of one another in heaps, exactly as if you were moving house, all on top of one another. I ask you. I could create a better show getting out of bed in the morning.

Image is everything – how things look on the outside, without worrying about the inside. There are plenty of smart clothes on the streets, but what's inside them is a different matter, not as substantial. You have to have a little Order with Freedom don't you? Don't you?

PAULINE – 5

LOOKING THROUGH HER PHOTOGRAPH ALBUM.

I've been sorting old black and white photos from school days, and when I showed them to Felicity I had to tell her that she was the only one still alive out of the people in some of them. I think she's afraid of looking at any more of them in case she thinks I'm giving her the kiss of death. Her reaction towards me was like going past those huge fridges in Marks and Spencers when I laughed out loud about it. She thought I was being too flippant.

PAULINE CLOSES THE ALBUM.

Last Sunday I went with the Conservative Club for a meal – we didn't go to the Tower Hotel this time because the meat was tough there last time. I had a trifle for pudding. The dinner plate was so hot I nearly threw it at Felicity. That would have finished her off! You've got to laugh at life.

I've got to be at Knutsford at half past six tomorrow morning to catch the Shearings to Brussels and Bruges. I'll be going by myself this time. I always think you meet more people that way.

PAULINE RISES FROM HER SEAT AND LOOKS OUT THROUGH THE WINDOW. CHILDREN CAN BE HEARD RUSHING ON THEIR WAY TO SCHOOL. SHE GAZES IMPASSIVELY THROUGH THE WINDOW. LIGHT FADES.

JAN – 5

When I see my ex in Town, I have to look the other way, 'cos we still love one another, and if he touched me I know that would be it. He knows he's been a soft bugger. He's fifty now and he wants a family – somethin' he could do without before – and the sad thing is his real family 'ave all grown up and gone. It's terrible – after twenty seven years of being together, suddenly it's as if your arm has been chopped off. It's exactly like that – there's a part of you that's gone for ever. I don't want him back, but I can't imagine a world without him in it somewhere. Even though he's been nasty to me – he did hit me – I know that he still loves me too.

JAN GIVES SOME WATER TO A PLANT ON THE DESK.

RYAN – 5

Selwyn, my old mate in the Foundry, comes over every morning from Southsea. Glanrafon he calls it – the old Welsh name on the village. He's a lot older than me, Selwyn, and the closure of the steel works was particularly difficult for him being on his own, like. It somehow stripped away his reason to live. So comin' here every mornin' for about two hours is good for 'im in his fifties. He still looks good, mind. Then we'll 'ave a coffee and a chat. I miss 'im when he doesn't come.

159

RYAN DOES SOME SIT UPS OR OTHER EXERCISE.

I'm back with Elaine now, but we haven't got married second time around. I pull my former brother-in-law's leg when I work out with 'im on the weights. Elaine comes to Keep Fit with my sister. We're all related up here whether you like it or not. There's no escape, so you just get on with it. CYHYRAU has brought us all back together again. The steel works was to blame for everythin' really – lives in ruts, and for a while I just 'ad to be free. It was the steel works closin' that gave me the chance to escape though. The only thing left of the Works now are the ghosts of the workers still workin' the Old Foundry – Selwyn's a bit of a poet. He says that you can still hear them workin' there in the dead of night.

I've realised now that it wasn't really running away from my wife that I wanted, but an escape from the rut. And after the steel works closed I discovered the steel in my own blood, and then I realised the benefits of the familiar things. But I did apologise to my wife for goin' to live with Lara, the young girl who used to cut me hair.

Selwyn is always singin' an old Welsh folk song

Ond cariad pur sydd fel y dur
  Yn para tra bo dau.

I know that **that** steel is there inside me now.

DAI OWEN – 6

I'm not sure if I should tell you this one in Chapel, but I can remember helpin' to smash the windows in Pant Mill. Five of us were called up before the teacher, one was given such a beating, so the others had their revenge. They pulled up all the plants and trees from his garden in Ruabon. They say that revenge is sweet, but it isn't. That's one thing I regret in my life. It's still with me. We were rum lads sometimes – followin' the railway from Pant to Plas Bennion because it was a short cut.

Another time I was meant to be in a Preaching Festival 'cos my Dad was big "chapel" but I wasn't in the *Cwarfod Pregethu uffen*. I was in the back of the Stiwt smokin'. Not as strong as these Capstan Full Strength I'm on now, enai. The teacher caught me next morning:

– *Lle oeddet ti neithiwr ?* **Where were you lad?**

– **In the Preaching Festival. Dad'll swear to it.**

Little white lies. I was a *cythraul* expectin' to go down the Pit at fourteen, and my father said "No, you're not goin' down the Hafod", and he sent me back to school. But I did work in Form Four and Five.

DAI COULD SLOT HYMN TUNE NUMBERS INTO A WOODEN DISPLAY, PREPARING FOR HIS LAST SERVICE.

JESSICA – 4

I'm not telling anyone about this letter to Dirk Bogarde, in case they say "What a silly little bitch!" At the start of the letter I tell him: I must refrain from my old habit of going on and on in letters. It's one thing saying that, but what do I do then? Go on and on for ten pages of huge writing paper, using both sides, and concluding with "Well, it seems that I can't keep my promises".

If I get a reply, the part of me that's a lady through and through will willingly respond – afternoon tea in the Savoy perhaps, that would be lovely. There's a lady under this skin waiting to get out you know – despite my socialist ideals. Dirk will have to decide for himself won't he?

I left a clear message on the back of the envelope: If undelivered, return it to Prozac Close. I haven't had a reply yet, so the letter must be somewhere. Hey, as soon as he gets it, I'm sure he'll be packing his bags for America – worrying incessantly about the effect he has on forlorn and frustrated middle-aged divorcees in their lonely flats. Perhaps he's escaped in case I demand my pound of flesh from him. Perhaps he thinks I'm like Glenn Close in Fatal Attraction. Thank God I've only got a shower in this flat. I wouldn't like a mess in the bath.

I expected the BBC to phone him and say

– Hey Dirk, there's a letter for you here. And then someone hands him my epic. The last time I wrote to someone famous was that cowboy from **Waggons Away** years ago – when I was thirteen. Come to think of it, I didn't get a reply from him either.

JAN – 6

JAN IS PLANTING BULBS IN A POT.

Before, in the house, everythin' was set out in the way he wanted – it was his furniture. Well, I've re-vamped it all, and it belongs to me now. I know he used to be a dab hand in the garden, but I've started to experiment. I've been to Woolies this mornin' to buy all these new seeds, and to look for the most beautiful flowers. It was 'im who used to do all this – beautiful hanging baskets. I was on the verge of pulling them all down 'cos they used to choke me with old memories, like a noose around my neck, hangin' there outside the door everytime I went out.

But I've kept the wooden window boxes for the flowers, cos he made them; and after all he was a good carpenter. And in the end I decided that there was still some good soil left in the hanging baskets as well, even though they'd been hangin' there barren for two years. And I thought -sod it – I must be feelin' better, 'cos I'm goin' to plant new seeds in 'em that'll flower in the Spring.

JAN FINGERS AND TENDS TO THE POT, MAKING SURE THAT SHE HAS WATERED IT PROPERLY.

DAI OWEN – 7

DAI RECITES THE POEM ABOUT THE WORKERS IN A PREACHER-STYLE VOICE.

> *Dringo i fyny mae y werin,*
> *Trwy galedi o bob rhyw,*
> *Tua gorsedd wen y nefoedd*
> *Lle teyrnasa cariad Duw.*
> *Mae ei lwybrau yn rhai celyd,*
> *Drain a dirmyg arnynt sydd,*
> *Ond er hynny cerdda'n araf*
> *Tua gwlad y bythol rydd.*

We were all working class heroes back then. Before I leave this old world, I must get hold of **Salmau'r Werin. The Commoner's Psalms**, but I can't for the life of me remember who wrote them.

I can hear Jim now.

– I shout in Welsh at the dog *Tshid yma uffen* or *Doro fyny*. Nobody understands Welsh in Town *ffwl*.

The echo of those few Welsh words from Jim are no longer to be heard late at night on Bradley Road. Old Jim.

Poverty hadn't beaten Jim – he owned his Ruabon red-brick terraced house in a secluded street in Town. He went to Rochdale in his teens, and then he came closer home, and was still in Rhos even though he lived in Wrexham, 'cos his memory lingered there. He came back to work in the Brick Works, then to Bersham, then on the

163

Grosville. He saw so much but he still remembered old characters like Bob Herrings. Jim was very serious about his memories. Every Thursday he'd be there in the Cafe, wearing his cap with that funny tassle.

– *Wyt ti'n cofio?* Do you remember?

Jim remembered things better than me, because he remembered things from the other side of the fence. *O ochor ene'r wal,* and that's why I admire Jim, and why I'm goin' to miss him. His stories about things going wrong in Capel Gobaith *"Ma'r Achos 'di bygro ene"*, and he remembers seeing the Policeman helping himself to some clothes when someone had broken into Siop Crecy. *Uffen*, Jim could tell 'em.

Perhaps I had the chance to learn a bit more English, and about Welsh literature and so on, but Jim had the history of Rhos on his lips, because he was the epitome of the true history of the village. He personified the worker, and there's none of his kind left in Rhos now, no matter how much Lottery money they get to restore it. That won't come back again. Jim was the last one, dying an exile in Town without anyone there to appreciate him. Rhos was the one place on earth where he was not deemed odd. *Y Werin Dlawd.* The noble worker. Not the ones who had an easy life – like me.

Well, there you have it – you've heard my last sermon. I'm going home now.

"Mi geisiaf eto ganu cân…"

I'm going to the rockin' chair by the fire anyway, and although I haven't got a lovely coal fire, the electric fire will suffice. Perhaps I'll dip into Dodd tonight and his history of the North East coalfield. I'll listen to it on the tape that Carwen has recorded for me, although I've got plenty of tapes in my head if it comes to that. Dodd's great work. You know he was the only good thing ever to come out of Coedpoeth! From *Gwlad y Derods, uffen*! It's not a book that you'll throw in the fire is it? And also I'll be thinking of Jim, and how I'll miss seeing him on Thursday afternoons from now on.

– *Wyt ti'n cofio Dai ?* **Do you remember Dai?** I only remember **you** tonight Jim, and I also know that memories are a man's best friend.

DAI STARTS HUMMING A HYMN TUNE (BERWYN) IN A DIGNIFIED MANNER. THE LIGHT FADES AS HE SINGS

"Pan fyddo'r don ar f'enaid gwan yn curo,
Mae'n dawel gyda Iesu wrth y Groes."